William Hunt

The English Church in the Middle Ages

William Hunt

The English Church in the Middle Ages

1st Edition | ISBN: 978-3-75238-337-9

Place of Publication: Frankfurt am Main, Germany

Year of Publication: 2020

Outlook Verlag GmbH, Germany.

THE ENGLISH CHURCH IN THE MIDDLE AGES.

BY

WILLIAM HUNT.

PREFACE.

This book is intended to illustrate the relations of the English Church with the papacy and with the English State down to the revolt of Wyclif against the abuses which had gathered round the ecclesiastical system of the Middle Ages, and the Great Schism in the papacy which materially affected the ideas of the whole of Western Christendom. It was thought expedient to deal with these subjects in a narrative form, and some gaps have therefore had to be filled up, and some links supplied. This has been done as far as possible by notices of matters which bear on the moral condition of the Church, and serve to show how far it was qualified at various periods to be the example and instructor of the nation. No attempt, however, has been made to write a complete history on a small scale, and I have designedly passed by many points, in themselves of interest and importance, in order to give as much space as might be to my proper subjects. Besides, this volume has been written as one of a series in which the missions to the Teutonic peoples, the various aspects of Monasticism, the question of Investitures, and the place which the University of Oxford fills in our Church's history have been, or will be, treated separately. Accordingly I have not touched on any of these things further than seemed absolutely necessary.

I wish that, limited as my task has been, I could believe that it has been adequately performed. No one can understand the character, or appreciate the claims, of the English Church who has not studied its history from the beginning, and it is hoped that this little book may do something, however small, towards spreading a correct idea of the part that the Church has borne in the progress of the nation, and of the grounds on which its members maintain that it has from the first been a National Church, as regards its inherent life and independent attitude as well as its intimate and peculiar relations with the State. A firm grasp of the position it held during the Middle Ages is necessary to a right understanding of the final rupture with Rome accomplished in the sixteenth century, and will afford a complete safeguard against the vulgar error of regarding the Church as a creation of the State, an institution established by the civil power, and maintained by its bounty. Those who are acquainted with our mediæval chroniclers will see that I have written from original sources. I have also freely availed myself of the labours of others, and, above all, of the works of Bishop Stubbs, which have been of the greatest assistance to me.

ARCHBISHOPS OF CANTERBURY TO 1377.

	Accession.	Death.
Augustin	597	604
Laurentius	604	619
Mellitus	619	624
Justus	624	627
Honorius	627	653
Deusdedit	655	664
Theodore	668	690
Brihtwald	693	731
Tatwin	731	734
Nothelm	735	739
Cuthberht	740	758
Brecgwin	759	765
Jaenberht	766	791
Æthelheard	793	805
Wulfred	805	832
Feologeld	832	832
Ceolnoth	833	870
Æthelred	870	889
Plegmund	890	914
Athelm	914	923
Wulfhelm	923	942
Oda	942	959
Dunstan	960	988
Æthelgar	988	989
Sigeric	990	994
Ælfric	995	1005
Ælfheah	1005	1012
Lyfing	1013	1020
Æthelnoth	1020	1038
Eadsige	1038	1050
Robert	1051	1070

Stigand	1052	...
Lanfranc	1070	1089
Anselm	1093	1109
Ralph	1114	1122
William of Corbeuil	1123	1136
Theobald	1139	1161
Thomas [Becket]	1162	1170
Richard	1174	1184
Baldwin	1185	1190
Hubert Walter	1193	1205
Stephen Langton	1207	1228
Richard Grant	1229	1231
Edmund Rich	1234	1240
Boniface	1245	1270
Robert Kilwardby	1273	res. 1278
John Peckham	1279	1292
Robert Winchelsey	1294	1313
Walter Reynolds	1313	1327
Simon Mepeham	1328	1333
John Stratford	1333	1348
Thomas Bradwardine	1349	1349
Simon Islip	1349	1366
Simon Langham	1366	res. 1368
William Whittlesey	1368	1374
Simon Sudbury	1375	1381

4

BISHOPS AND ARCHBISHOPS OF YORK TO 1377.

	Accession.	Death.
Paulinus	625	…
Wilfrith	664	709
Ceadda	664	res. 669
Bosa	678	705
John of Beverley	705	res. 718
Wilfrith II.	718	732
Ecgberht	732	766
Æthelberht (Albert)	766	780
Eanbald	780	796
Eanbald II.	796	812
Wulfsige	…	831
Wigmund	837	…
Wulfhere	854	900
Æthelbald	900	…
Redewald	cir. 928	…
Wulfstan	cir. 931	956
Oskytel	958	971
Oswald	972	992
Ealdulf	992	1002
Wulfstan II.	1003	1023
Ælfric	1023	1051
Kinesige	1051	1060
Ealdred	1060	1069
Thomas	1070	1100
Gerard	1101	1108
Thomas II.	1109	1114
Thurstan	1119	1140
William	1143	1154
Henry Murdac	1147	1153
Roger	1154	1181

Geoffrey	1191	1212
Walter Gray	1215	1255
Sewal de Bovill	1256	1258
Godfrey	1258	1265
Walter Giffard	1266	1279
William Wickwain	1279	1285
John le Roman	1286	1296
Henry Newark	1298	1299
Thomas Corbridge	1300	1303
William Greenfield	1306	1315
William Melton	1317	1340
William Zouche	1342	1352
John Thoresby	1352	1373
Alexander Neville	1374	1392

CHAPTER I.

ROME AND IONA.

ST. AUGUSTIN'S MISSION—POPE GREGORY'S SCHEME OF ORGANIZATION—CAUSES OF ITS FAILURE—FOUNDATION AND OVERTHROW OF THE SEE OF YORK —INDEPENDENT MISSIONS—THE SEE OF LINDISFARNE—SCOTTISH CHRISTIANITY—THE SCHISM— THE SYNOD OF WHITBY— RESTORATION OF THE SEE OF YORK.

The Gospel was first brought to the Teutonic conquerors of Britain by Roman missionaries, and was received by the kings of various kingdoms. From the first the Church that was planted here was national in character, and formed a basis for national union; and when that union was accomplished the English State became coextensive with the English Church, and was closely united with it. The main object of this book is to trace the relations of the Church both with the Papacy and with the State down to the new era that opened with the schism in the Papacy and the Wyclifite movement. St. Augustin's landing at Ebbsfleet, 597.Our narrative will begin with the coming of Augustin and his companions in 597 to preach the Gospel to the English people. They landed in the Isle of Thanet. The way had, to some extent, been prepared for them, for Æthelberht, king of Kent, whose superiority was acknowledged as far north as the Humber, had married a Christian princess named Bertha, the daughter of a Frankish king, and had allowed her to bring a priest with her and to practise her own religion. He had not, however, learnt much about Christianity from his queen or her priest. Nevertheless, he received the Gospel from Augustin, and was baptized with many of his people. By Gregory's command, Augustin was consecrated "archbishop of the English nation" by the archbishop of Arles. Æthelberht gave him his royal city of Canterbury, and built for him there the monastery of Christ Church, the mother-church of ourcountry.

Gregory's scheme of organization, 601.

Gregory organized the new Church, in the full belief that it would extend over the whole island. He sent Augustin the "pall," a vestment denoting metropolitan authority, and constituting the recipient vicar of the Pope. Two metropolitan sees were to be established—the one at London, the residence of the East Saxon King Sæberct, who reigned as sub-king under Æthelberht, a crowded mart, and the centre of a system of roads; the other at York, the capital of the old Roman province north of the Humber. Both archbishops were to receive the pall, and to be of equal authority. At the same time, the unity of the Church was ensured, for they were to consult together and act in unison. Both the provinces were to be divided into twelve suffragan bishoprics, and as the northern province took in the country now called Scotland, they were of fairly equal size. This arrangement was not to be carried out until after Augustin's death. As long as he lived all the bishops alike were to obey him, and he was, we may suppose, to continue to reside at Canterbury. Moreover, the clergy of the Welsh or Britons were to be subject to him and to the future archbishops of the English Church. Augustin endeavoured to persuade the Welsh clergy to join him in preaching the Gospel to the Teutonic invaders, and held a meeting with them at or near Aust, on the Severn. But they refused to acknowledge his authority, or even to hold communion with him, and would not give up their peculiar usages with respect to the date of Easter and the administration of Baptism. At Augustin's request, Gregory sent him a letter of instructions as to the government of the Church. It bears witness to the Pope's largeness of mind. While morality and decency were to be enforced, the archbishop was not bound strictly to follow the Roman ritual; if he found anything that he thought would be helpful to his converts in the Gallican or any other use, he might adopt it, and so make up a use collected from various sources.

Causes of
its failure.

Excellent as Gregory's scheme would have been had Britain still been under Roman rule, it was unsuited to a country divided as England then was into several rival kingdoms. London did not become a metropolitan see, probably because Æthelberht was unwilling that the seat of ecclesiastical authority should be transferred from his own kingdom to the chief city of a dependent people, while Augustin had no wish that the church which he had founded at Canterbury, and the second monastery, now called after him, which he had begun to build there for a burying-place for himself and his successors, should be reduced to a lower rank. Other Roman clergy had been sent by Gregory to reinforce the mission, and of these Augustin consecrated Mellitus to be bishop of London, Justus to be bishop over Kent west of the Medway, with Rochester as the city of his see, an arrangement that marks an early tribal distinction, and Laurentius to be his own successor at Canterbury. Thus the metropolitan see remained with Kent. More generally, Gregory's scheme failed because it was founded on the old division of Britain as a province of the Roman empire, and was not adapted to the tribal distinctions of the English. Moreover, political circumstances determined the development of the Church; for the Roman mission received a series of checks, and the work of evangelization was taken up by Scottish missionaries. The kingdoms into which the country was divided were finally converted by efforts more or less independent of the Kentish mission; the work of evangelization followed tribal lines, and for sixty years after Augustin's death the tendency of the Church was towards disunion.

Although the king of the East Angles received baptism in Kent at the bidding of Æthelberht, he fell back into idolatry on his return to his own land. And as Æthelberht's son, Eadbald, was a pagan, many of the Kentishmen and East Saxons also deserted Christianity when he became king. Eadbald was converted by Laurentius, and did what he could to forward the cause of Christ. With Æthelberht's death, however, the greatness of Kent passed away, and Eadbald could not insist on the destruction of idols even in his own country. While Kent sank into political insignificance the Kentish mission made one great advance, and then ended in failure. Foundation and overthrow of the see of York, 627-633. The Northumbrian king, Eadwine, who reigned over the two Northumbrian kingdoms, Bernicia and Deira, from the Forth to the Humber, and gradually established a supremacy over the whole English people except the Kentishmen, married Æthelburh, the daughter of Æthelberht. She was accompanied to her new home by Paulinus, who was ordained bishop by Justus, the successor of Mellitus; and Boniface V. wrote to her exhorting her to labour for the conversion of her husband, and saying that he would not cease to pray for her success. His prayers were heard; Eadwine was baptized, and made his capital, York, the seat of the bishopric of Paulinus. The people of Deira (Yorkshire) followed their king's example, while Bernicia, though Paulinus preached and baptized there, remained, on the whole, heathen; no church was built and no altar was raised. South of the Humber the authority of Eadwine and the preaching of Paulinus effected the conversion of Lindsey, and of the king, at least, of the East Angles. In 633, however, Eadwine was defeated and slain by Penda, the heathen king of Mercia, and Cadwallon, the Briton. Heathenism was already triumphant in East Anglia, and on Eadwine's death many of the Northumbrians relapsed into idolatry. Æthelburh and her children sought shelter in Kent, and Paulinus fled with them. Only one Roman clergyman, the deacon James, remained in Northumbria to labour on in faith that God's cause would yet triumph there. Ignorant of the calamity that had befallen the Church, the Pope, in pursuance of Gregory's scheme, sent the pall to Paulinus. When the papal gift arrived in England the Church of York had been overthrown, and Paulinus had been translated to Rochester.

Independent
missions.

After the success of the Kentish mission had received this terrible check, the work of evangelization was carried on by efforts that were more or less independent of it. East Anglia was finally converted by a Burgundian priest named Felix, who was consecrated bishop by Honorius, archbishop of Canterbury, and fixed his see at Dunwich, once on the Suffolk coast. The Italian, Birinus, who was consecrated in Italy, brought the Gospel to the West Saxons, and received Dorchester, in Oxfordshire, for the place of his see. Northumbria was evangelized by Celtic missionaries who were not in communion with Rome and Canterbury. About the middle of the sixth century the Irish Scot, Columba, founded the monastery of Iona. He and his companions preached the Gospel to the northern Picts and the Scots of the western isles, and Iona became a centre of Christian light. During the reign of Eadwine, Oswald and Oswiu, princes of the rival Bernician line, had found shelter in Iona. Oswald returned to become king of Bernicia shortly after the death of Eadwine, and before long brought Deira also under his dominion. As soon as he had gained possession of the kingdom of Bernicia, he sent to Iona for missionaries to instruct his people. Aidan, a missionary from Columba's house, came to him, and so it came to pass that Bernicia received Christianity from Celtic teachers, from Aidan and his fellow-workers. Foundation of the see of Lindisfarne, 635. Oswald warmly seconded their efforts, and fixed the see of Aidan, who was in bishop's orders, in Lindisfarne, or Holy Isle, not far from Bamborough, where he resided; for though he ruled over both the Northumbrian kingdoms, and completed the minster at York, he made his home in the North, among his own people. Bernicia thus became the stronghold of Celtic Christianity under the rule of the kings of the house of Ida, while the Christians of Deira were naturally more inclined to the Roman usages which had been introduced by Paulinus and practised by Eadwine and his queen. Aidan built a monastery at Lindisfarne, and peopled it with monks from Iona. This gave him a good supply of clergy, and the work of evangelization prospered and took deep root. The greatness of Oswald provoked Penda to renew his struggle with the northern kingdom, and the Northumbrian king was defeated and slain at Maserfield. As his foes closed round him he prayed for their conversion. His words sank deeply into men's hearts. "'May God have mercy on their souls,' said Oswald, as he fell to earth," was a line handed down from generation to generation. From his hermit's retreat on Farne Island, Aidan beheld the thick clouds of smoke rise from the country round Bamborough, and cried, "Behold, Lord, the evil that Penda doeth!" Still the work of God went on; and when Oswiu came to the

10

throne the prayer of Oswald received its answer, for a marriage between his house and the house of Penda led to the evangelization of the Mercians and Middle Angles by the monks of Iona. From them too the East Saxons received the Gospel, and Cedd, an English monk of Lindisfarne, was consecrated to the bishopric that had been held by the Roman Mellitus.

By the middle of the seventh century only Kent and East Anglia remained in full and exclusive communion with Rome; for Sussex was still heathen, Wini, the West Saxon bishop, acted with British bishops, and Scottish Christianity prevailed in all the rest of England. The Scottish missionaries were full of zeal and self-devotion, and were masters of a considerable store of learning. Their nature was impulsive; while they were loving and tender-hearted, passionate invectives came as readily from their lips as words of love. Celtic Christianity was a religion of perpetual miracles, of deep and varying emotions, and of contempt for worldly things, that, however noble in itself, was sometimes manifested extravagantly. While its teachers seldom failed to win men's love, they were not equally successful in influencing their conduct. It was well that the English Church turned away from them, for their religious system could never have produced an organized ecclesiastical society. It was monastic rather than hierarchical, and a Celtic priest-abbot was a far more important person than a bishop who was not the ruler of an abbey, though in England the bishops were probably always abbots. In founding their sees they sought seclusion rather than good administrative centres, and the bishop's monastery was less a place of diocesan government than the headquarters of missionary effort. They had no regular diocesan system, and bishops and clergy ministered where they would. Their monasticism was of a specially ascetic character. Both Aidan and Cuthberht loved to leave the society of the monks at Lindisfarne, and to retire to the barren little Farne Island, where they could only hear the roaring of the northern ocean and the crying of the sea-birds. Cuthberht, indeed, even after he joined the Roman Church, kept the characteristics of the Scottish monk. He left the duties of his bishopric altogether and ended his days in his island-hermitage. This love of asceticism was fatal to the well-being of the Church; the individual soul was everything; the Church was nothing; and though great victories were won over heathenism, the Scottish Church remained without corporate life. Lastly, it was not in communion with Rome, and so lay outside Catholic Christendom. And though it had much to offer the English both in religion and learning, every gift would have been rendered fruitless by isolation from the progressive life of Western Christendom.

It was, indeed, impossible, from the very nature of things, that Celtic Christianity should long prevail in England, for its arrangements were based on the loose organization of the sept, and the English needed arrangements that suited kingship and tended towards political as well as ecclesiastical union. Its rejection was, however, determined by questions of Church order. Up to the middle of the fifth century the Celtic Christians computed Easter by the Roman lunar cycle, which had gradually diverged from that of Eastern Christendom. When, however, the Romans adopted a new system of computation, the Welsh and the Irish Scots adhered to the old cycle; and they further differed from the Roman Church as regards the shape of the tonsure and the rites observed in the administration of Baptism. Unimportant as such differences may seem to us, they were really no light matters; for, as the Church was engaged in a conflict with paganism, unity with itself was of the first consequence. The points at issue began to be much debated in Northumbria when the gentle-spirited Aidan was succeeded at Lindisfarne by Finan, a man of violent temper. The Bernician court was divided. Oswiu was attached to the Scottish communion, and his attachment was strengthened by his regard for Colman, the successor of Finan. On the other hand, his queen, Eanflæd, the daughter of Eadwine, belonged to the Roman party; and so it came about that, while the king was keeping his Easter feast, his queen was still in the Lenten fast. Oswiu's son, Alchfrith, who reigned as under-king in Deira, left the Scottish communion and eagerly upheld the Roman party. He was encouraged by Wilfrith, the abbot of Ripon. Wilfrith, who was the child of wealthy parents, had been led by the unkindness of his stepmother to desire to become a monk, and had been sent, when a handsome, clever lad of thirteen, to Queen Eanflæd, that she might decide what he should do. Eanflæd sent him to Lindisfarne, and he stayed there for some years. Then she helped him to visit Rome, and he made the journey, which was as yet unknown to his fellow-countrymen, partly in the company of Benedict Biscop, who became the founder of Roman monasticism in the north of England. While he was at Rome Wilfrith studied ecclesiastical matters, and especially the subject of the computation of Easter. He returned home fully convinced of the excellence of the Roman Church, and found in Alchfrith a warm friend and willing disciple. Alchfrith had built a monastery at Ripon, and peopled it with Scottish monks from Melrose. When he adopted the Roman customs, these monks, of whom Cuthberht was one, refused to follow his example, and accordingly he turned them out, and gave the monastery to Wilfrith.

12

Before long Wilfrith, who was a good preacher and charitable to the poor, became exceedingly popular. The ecclesiastical dispute was evidently closely connected with the rivalry between the two Northumbrian kingdoms; the Roman cause was upheld in Deira and by the Deiran under-king, while the Celtic clergy were strong in Bernicia, and trusted in the support of Oswiu. A visit from Agilberct, a Frank, who had held the West Saxon bishopric, and had since returned to Gaul, gave Alchfrith an opportunity of bringing matters to an issue. Agilberct admitted Wilfrith to the priesthood, and urged on a decision of the dispute. A conference was held at the abbey of Strenæshalch, or Whitby. The abbey was ruled by Hild, great-niece of King Eadwine, who presided over a congregation composed of monks as well as nuns. Five of Hild's monks became bishops, and the poet Cædmon was first a herdsman, and then a brother of her house. Hild belonged to the Scottish party, which was represented at the conference by Colman, Cedd, and others. The leaders on the Roman side were Agilberct, Wilfrith, James the deacon of Paulinus, and Eanflæd's chaplain, Romanus. The question was decided in a synod of the whole Northumbrian kingdom, presided over by Oswiu and Alchfrith. Oswiu opened the proceedings with a short speech, in which he urged the necessity of union and the importance of finding out what the true tradition was. Colman then stated his case, which he rested on the tradition of his Church and the authority of St. John. At the request of Agilberct, Oswiu called on Wilfrith to answer him. Wilfrith spoke in an overbearing tone, for he was of an impatient temper. He sneered at the obstinacy of "a few Picts and Britons" in setting themselves in opposition to the whole world, and met Colman's arguments by declaring that the Celtic Easter was condemned by St. Peter, of whom the Lord had said, "Thou art Peter," &c. (Matt. xvi. 18). On this, Oswiu asked Colman whether the Lord had indeed spoken thus, and when he said that He had done so, further demanded whether his Columba had received any such power. Colman allowed that he had not. The king then asked whether both parties were agreed that Peter had received the keys of Heaven. "Even so," was the answer. "Then," said he, "I will not go against him who is doorkeeper, but will do all I know and can to obey him, lest perchance, when I come to the door of the kingdom of Heaven, I should find none to open to me, because he who holds the keys is offended with me." The assembly agreed with the king's decision, and declared for the Roman usages. James the deacon saw the reward of his long and faithful labour; he was a skilful singer, and introduced the Roman method of chanting into Northumbria.

The Synod of Whitby is the turning-point in the history of the schism. Before many years the Celtic party died out in the north, and though the Celtic customs lingered a little longer among the Britons of the west, the decisive blow had been struck; the Church of England was to follow Rome. The gain was great. The Church was to have a share in the progressive life of Catholic Christianity; it was to have a stately ritual, and to be adorned by the arts and strengthened by the learning of the west; it gained unity and organization for itself, and the power of exercising a determining influence on the lives of individual men, and on the formation and history of the future State. Nevertheless, the decision of the synod was not all gain, for it led to the submission of the Church to papal authority, and in times of national weakness exposed it to papal aggression.

Restoration
of the see of
York, 664.

Colman refused to accept the decision of the synod, and left England in anger, taking several of his monks with him. His departure ruined the cause of his Church. His successor in the vast Northumbrian diocese died of the terrible plague that visited England the year of the Synod. Then the two kings held a meeting of the Northumbrian witan, and Wilfrith was chosen bishop. The victory of his party was further declared by the restoration of the see of York. Ever since the flight of Paulinus, York had remained without a bishop; now, doubtless at the instance of Alchfrith and the people of Deira, it took the place of Bernician Lindisfarne as the seat of the Northumbrian bishopric. Wilfrith went to Gaul to receive consecration, on the ground that there were not three canonically ordained bishops in England, an assertion which seems to have been hasty and incorrect. He stayed abroad for three years, and so well-nigh threw away the victory he had gained, for while he was absent Alchfrith lost his kingdom, and the rivalry between the two divisions of Northumbria found expression in a revulsion of feeling in ecclesiastical matters. When he came back he found that Aidan's disciple, Ceadda (St. Chad), the brother of Cedd, who had adopted the Roman customs, had been appointed bishop in his place. He retired to Ripon, acted as bishop in other parts, and helped forward the introduction of Roman monasticism into monasteries that had hitherto followed the Columban model.

CHAPTER II.

ORGANIZATION.

ARCHBISHOP THEODORE—HIS WORK IN ORGANIZATION—NEW DIOCESES—WILFRITH'S APPEALS TO ROME—LITERARY GREATNESS OF NORTHUMBRIA—PARISHES—TITHES—THE CHURCH IN WESSEX —A THIRD ARCHBISHOPRIC—THE CHURCH IN RELATION TO THE STATE—TO ROME—TO WESTERN CHRISTENDOM.

Archbishop
Theodore,
668-690.

Among the victims of the plague of 664 was Archbishop Deusdedit, the first English successor of Augustin. After the see of Canterbury had lain vacant for three years, Oswiu, who held a kind of supremacy in England, and Ecgberht of Kent joined in writing to Pope Vitalian, asking him to consecrate a Kentish priest named Wighard as archbishop. Wighard died of the plague at Rome before he was consecrated, and the Pope wrote to the kings that, agreeably to their request, he was looking for a fit man to be consecrated. As, however, the kings had made no such request, and had simply asked him to consecrate the man whom they and the English Church had chosen, his letter was more clever than honest. He made choice of a Greek monk, a native of Tarsus, named Theodore, who had joined the Roman Church; and as the Greeks held unorthodox opinions, he sent with him Hadrian, an African, abbot of the Niridan monastery, near Naples, that he might prevent him from teaching any wrong doctrines. Theodore was consecrated by the Pope in 668, and set out for England with Hadrian and Benedict Biscop, of whom much will be said in the volume of this series on monasticism. Both Theodore and Hadrian were learned men, and the archbishop gathered round him a number of students, whom they instructed in arts and sciences as well as in Biblical knowledge. They also taught Latin and Greek so thoroughly that some of their scholars spoke both languages as readily as English, and for the first time England had a learned native clergy. Many of their scholars became teachers of others, and in the darkest period of ignorance in Gaul, England, and especially Northumbria, entered on a period of literary splendour that lasted until the

15

Danish invasions.

As the Church was now rapidly passing from the missionary to the pastoral stage of its existence, it needed organization as a permanent institution. This organization was given to it by Theodore. He established his authority over the whole Church, and, long before any one thought of a national monarchy, planned a national archiepiscopate. He made a visitation of every see, and for the first time every bishop owned obedience to Canterbury; while, as far as the English were concerned, he virtually brought the schism to an end by enforcing the decision of the Synod of Whitby. When he came to York he told Ceadda that his consecration was uncanonical. The saintly bishop declared his readiness to resign; he had ever, he said, deemed himself unworthy of the episcopal office. Theodore was touched by his humility, and reordained him; he received the Mercian bishopric, and lived for a little while in great holiness at Lichfield. Wilfrith was restored to York, and ruled his diocese with magnificence. When Theodore had thus established his authority, he proceeded to give the Church a diocesan system and a means of legislation in ecclesiastical matters. He called a national council of the Church to meet at Hertford; it was attended by the bishops and several "masters of Church," men learned in ecclesiastical affairs, and in it the archbishop produced a body of canons which were universally accepted. These canons declared that the Roman Easter was to be observed everywhere; that no bishop should intrude into another's diocese; that no priest should minister out of his own diocese without producing letters of recommendation; that a synod of the whole Church should be held every year at Clevesho, probably near London; and that more bishops were needed, a matter which it was decided to defer for the present.

Creation of
new
dioceses.

Instead of the symmetrical arrangement contemplated by Gregory, certain bishoprics were of immense size, for the diocese in each case was simply the kingdom looked at from an ecclesiastical point of view, and as the boundaries of a kingdom were changed by the fortune of war the diocese was enlarged or diminished. The whole of Central England was included in the one Mercian diocese, and the whole of Northumbria—for Lindisfarne was now without a separate bishop—lay in the diocese of Wilfrith. Theodore saw that it was necessary to subdivide these and other dioceses, and his intention was approved at Rome. His plan of procedure was first to gain the approval of the king whose kingdom would be affected by the change he wished to make, and then to obtain the consent of the witan. Hitherto the dioceses had been based on political circumstances; the new dioceses were generally formed on tribal lines. He divided East Anglia into two dioceses. The North folk and the South folk each had a bishop of their own, and the new see was placed at Elmham. Mercia was divided into five dioceses; the Hwiccan, the Hecanan, the Mercians proper, the Middle Angles, and the Lindsey folk each received a bishop, and the five sees were respectively at Worcester, Hereford, Lichfield, Leicester, and Sidnacester. The division of the West Saxon see was put off until the death of the bishop. In dealing with the Northumbrian diocese King Ecgfrith and the archbishop seem to have expected opposition from Wilfrith, for they divided his diocese in a council at which he was not present. According to the plan then adopted, Theodore consecrated bishops for Deira, Bernicia, and Lindsey, which, though originally part of the Mercian diocese, had lately been added to the Northumbrian kingdom and bishopric by conquest.

Wilfrith's
first appeal
to Rome,
678.

Wilfrith appeared before the king and the archbishop, and demanded to be told why he was thus deprived of his rights. No answer was given him, and he appealed to the judgment of the Apostolic See. This appeal to Rome against the decision of a king and his witan, and of an archbishop acting in concert, the first that was ever made by an Englishman, is a notable event. It was greeted with the jeers of the great men of the court. Wilfrith went to Rome in person, and Theodore appeared by a proctor. Pope Agatho and his council decreed that Wilfrith should be reinstated, that his diocese should be divided, but that he should choose the new bishops, and that Theodore's bishops should be turned out. Wilfrith returned in triumph, bringing the papal decrees with their bulls (seals) attached. A witenagemót was held to hear them, and the king and his nobles decided to disregard them. Wilfrith was imprisoned, and Theodore made a further division of his diocese by establishing a see at Abercorn, and appointed bishops for Lindisfarne, Hexham, and perhaps Ripon without consulting him. After Wilfrith was released he was forced by the hatred of Ecgfrith to wander about seeking shelter, until at last he found it among the heathen South Saxons. He converted them to Christianity, and lived as their bishop at Selsey. Then he preached to the people of the Isle of Wight, and by their conversion completed the work that Augustin came to do. The death of Ecgfrith made it possible for Theodore to come to terms with him. The archbishop and the injured bishop were reconciled in 686, and at Theodore's request Ealdfrith, the new king of Northumbria, reinstated Wilfrith as bishop of York. Nevertheless the division that Theodore had made was not disturbed, and he only presided over the Deiran diocese. He is driven from York a second time, 691.After some years he and Ealdfrith had a dispute about the rights and possessions of his see. He was again driven from York, and again appealed to Rome. Pope Sergius took his part. But Ealdfrith, though a religious man, was not more inclined to submit to papal interference than his predecessor. He found an ally in Archbishop Brihtwald, for Theodore was now dead, and in spite of the Pope's mandates, Wilfrith's claims were rejected by a national synod of the Church. He again appealed to Rome, and was excommunicated by the English bishops. Again he journeyed to Rome, and John VI. pronounced a decree in his favour. Ealdfrith, however, declared that he would never change his decision for papal writings, and it was not until after his death that a compromise was effected in a Northumbrian synod held on the Nidd in 705. Dies bishop of Hexham, 709.The settlement was unfavourable to Wilfrith, for he was not restored to York, but ended his days as bishop of Hexham. He was a man of blameless life and indomitable courage. It was mainly through his efforts that the Church of England was brought into conformity with the Roman Church. Defeat never made him idle or despondent, and his noblest triumphs, the conversion of the last heathen people of English race, were won in exile. At the same time, he was hasty, impolitic, and perhaps over-jealous for his own honour. In the part that the two archbishops took against him it is hard not to see some fear lest the magnificence of the northern prelate should endanger the authority of Canterbury in Northumbria, though they certainly acted for the good of the Church in insisting on the division of his vast diocese. He made the first attempt to control English ecclesiastical affairs by invoking the appellate jurisdiction of the Pope, and his defeat was the first of the many checks that papal interference received from Englishmen.

Literary
greatness of
Northumbria,
664-782.
Cædmon, d.
680.
Æddi
[Eddius], fl.
710.
Bæda, 673-
735.

From the time of its conversion by Aidan to its devastation by the Scandinavian pirates, Northumbria excelled the rest of England in arts and literature. Another volume of this series will deal with the famous monasteries of Lindisfarne, Jarrow, Wearmouth, Whitby, and York, with their scholar-monks, and with the splendours of Roman and Gallic art with which their churches were enriched. While Celtic culture was on the point of yielding to Roman influence, Cædmon, the herdsman, the first of our sacred poets, began to sing at Whitby. His story illustrates the love of the English for music; and this national characteristic caused the introduction of the Roman system of chanting to hold an important place in the process of bringing the Church into conformity with Rome. This part of the work of James the deacon was carried on by Æddi, a choirmaster of Canterbury, whom Wilfrith invited into Northumbria. Æddi became the bishop's companion, and wrote a "Life of Wilfrith," a work of considerable value. Shortly afterwards Bæda composed his "Ecclesiastical History." Bæda was absolutely free from narrowness of mind, and though he held that the Roman tradition was authoritative, loved and venerated the memory of the holy men of the Celtic Church. As a story-teller he is unrivalled: full of piety and tenderness, he preserved through life a simplicity of heart that invests his narratives with a peculiar grace. At the same time, he did all in his power to find out the exact truth, and constantly tells his readers where he derived his information. He was well read in the best Latin authors, and in patristic divinity; he understood Greek, and had some acquaintance with Hebrew. Besides his works on the Bible and his historical and biographical books, he wrote treatises on chronology, astronomy, mathematics, and music. From boyhood he spent all his life in the monastery of Jarrow in religious exercises and in literary labours, that he undertook not for his own sake, but for the sake of others. During his last sickness he worked hard to finish his translation of the Gospel of St. John, for he knew that it would be useful to his scholars. His last day on earth was spent upon it; and when evening came, and the young scribe said, "There is yet one more sentence, dear master, to be written out," he answered, "Write quickly." After a while the lad said, "Now the sentence is written;" and he answered, "Good; thou hast spoken truly. It is finished." Then he bade him raise his head, for he wished to look on the spot where he was wont to pray. And so, lying on the pavement of his cell, he sang the *Gloria Patri*, and as he uttered the name of the Holy Ghost he passed to the heavenly kingdom.

One of Bæda's friends was Ecgberht, who was made bishop of York in 734, and obtained the restoration of the metropolitan dignity of his see. A year after his election Bæda sent him a letter of advice which tells us a good deal about the state of the Church. While the work of evangelization was still going on, monasteries were useful as missionary centres, and a single church served for a large district. Now, however, men no longer needed missionary preachers so much as resident priests and regular services. Parishes.Accordingly, the parochial system came into existence about this time, not by any formal enactment, but in the natural course of things. For, when the lord of a township built a church, and had a priest ordained to minister to his people, his township in most cases became an ecclesiastical district or parish. Bæda urges the bishop to forward this change. He points out that it was impossible for him to visit every place in his diocese even once a year, and exhorts him to ordain priests to preach, to consecrate the Holy Mysteries, and to baptize in each village. The parish priest mainly subsisted on land assigned to him by the lord who built the church and on the offerings of the people, such as church-scot, which was paid at Martinmas, soul-scot or mortuary dues, and the like. These payments were obligatory, and were enjoined first by the law of the Church, and then by the civil power. It is evident from Bæda's letter that, even before the parochial system was established, a compulsory payment of some kind was made to the bishop by all the people of his diocese. Tithes.From the earliest times, also, the consecration of a tenth, or tithe, to the service of God was held to be a Christian duty, and the obligation is recognized in Theodore's Penitential, and was therefore part of the law of the Church. It became part of the civil law in 787, for it was then enjoined by a council presided over by two legates, and the decree was accepted by the kings and the witan of the kingdoms they visited. It is probable, however, that payment was not enforced till a later period. Early in the tenth century the obligation was recognized as an established law, and a penalty was provided for its non-fulfilment. The appropriation of the payment long remained unsettled, and was generally decided by the owner of the land, who in most cases naturally assigned the tithe to the parish priest, though he sometimes gave it to the head church of the district, or to the bishop's church, or to some monastery. And although the right of the parochial clergy to the tithe of increase was declared in 1200 by the Council of Westminster, the constitution was often evaded.

Restoration
   of the
archbishopric
   of York,
   734.

Many monasteries had in Bæda's time fallen into an evil condition, and as the Church needed an efficient diocesan organization, he advised Ecgberht to strive for the fulfilment of Pope Gregory's scheme as regards the Church in the north, which provided that the see of York should be metropolitan, and that the province should be divided into twelve bishoprics. The new bishops should, he proposed, be supported out of the funds of monasteries, which were in some cases to be placed under episcopal rule. In the same year that this letter was written, Ecgberht received the pall from Gregory III., and this grant, which had not been made to any of his predecessors since the time of Paulinus, restored the see to metropolitan dignity. Thus one part of Theodore's work was frustrated, and Northumbria was withdrawn from the jurisdiction of the see of Canterbury. The kingdom itself was withdrawing from the contests between the other English states, and the restoration of the archbishopric may be regarded as a kind of declaration of its separate national life. Under Ecgberht and his successor, Æthelberht (Albert), the Northumbrian Church was famous for learning, and the archbishop's school at York became the most notable place of education in Western Christendom. Æthelberht's schoolmaster was Alcuin, who after the archbishop's death resided at the court of Charles the Great, and helped him to carry out his plans for the advancement of learning. Alcuin had himself been a scholar at York, and so the school there became a source of light to other lands. In York itself, however, the light was quenched before Alcuin's death. Civil disturbances were followed by the Scandinavian invasions, and the Northumbrian Church for a long period almost disappears amidst anarchy and ruin.

Ealdhelm,
bishop of
Sherborne,
died 709.

In Wessex the work of Theodore was carried on by Ealdhelm, abbot of Malmesbury, one of his most distinguished scholars. Ini, the West Saxon king, had conquered the western part of Somerset, and ruled over a mixed population. The bitter feelings engendered by the schism were an hindrance to the Church in the west, and Ealdhelm wrote a treatise on the subject in the form of a letter to Gerent, king of Dyfnaint, which brought a number of the Welsh within the West Saxon border to conform to the customs of the Roman Church. This put an end to the schism in the west. In our present Wales the Roman Easter was universally accepted about a century later. Ealdhelm, who was a kinsman of Ini, was much honoured by the king, and used his influence to further the spread of the Gospel. Churches rose rapidly in Wessex, and he journeyed to Rome to obtain privileges for the monasteries he had founded, and was received with much kindness by Pope Sergius. The division of the West Saxon diocese which had been contemplated by Theodore took place in Ini's reign, and was settled by the king and an ecclesiastical council. All to the west of Selwood Forest, the western part of Wiltshire, Dorset, and Somerset formed the new diocese of Sherborne, and over this Ealdhelm was chosen bishop. The rest of Wessex remained in the diocese of Winchester, which had now taken the place of Dorchester as an episcopal see. The labours of Ealdhelm, and the help he received from his wise and powerful kinsman, brought about the extension and organization of the Church in the west. After raising Wessex to the foremost place among the kingdoms south of the Humber, Ini laid down his crown, made a pilgrimage to Rome, and died there.

The
archbishopric

of Lichfield,
786-802.

In the latter half of the eighth century Offa, king of Mercia, was the most powerful monarch in England, and, among other conquests, subdued Kent and added it to his dominions. The course of political events tended to a threefold division of England into the Northumbrian, Mercian, and West Saxon kingdoms, and the twofold system of ecclesiastical administration by the metropolitans of Canterbury and York thwarted the ambition of the Mercian king. Northumbria had already sealed its policy of separation by the restoration of the archbishopric of York, and Offa now adopted a similar course, by persuading Pope Hadrian I. to grant the see of Lichfield metropolitan dignity. He had a special reason for weakening the power of Canterbury, for after the extinction of Kentish royalty the archbishop gained increased political importance, and became the representative of the national life of the kingdom, which Offa vainly endeavoured to crush. Accordingly two legates of Hadrian held a synod at Chelsea in 787, in which Higberht, bishop of Lichfield, was declared an archbishop. Jaenberht, archbishop of Canterbury, was forced to submit to the partition of his province, the obedience of the Mercian and East Anglian bishops being apparently transferred to the new metropolitan.

This arrangement was subversive of a part of Theodore's work that was specially valuable as regards the development both of the Church and the nation. Theodore had made ecclesiastical jurisdictions independent of the fluctuations of political boundaries, and had freed the Church from provincial influences and from a merely local character. The national character of the Church was to become a powerful factor in forming the English nation. In spite of civil divisions, the oneness of the Church was a strong element of union. Although no lay assembly, no witenagemót, of the whole nation was as yet possible, the Church met in national councils; its head, the archbishop of Canterbury, might be a native of any kingdom, and every one of its clergy, of whatever race he might be, was equally at home in whatever part of the land he was called to minister. This national character of the Church and the influence it exercised on national unity were endangered by creating metropolitan jurisdiction and dignity as mere appendages to a political division. Happily there was no second archbishop of Lichfield. Offa's successor, Cenwulf, found Æthelheard, the archbishop of Canterbury, a useful ally in a revolt of the Kentish nobles, and joined him in obtaining the restoration of the rights of his see from Leo III. While the see of York was overwhelmed by political disasters, the archbishop of Canterbury gained increased importance. Wessex entered on a career of conquest under Ecgberht, who, in 827, defeated the Mercian king at Ellandun. This victory

22

led to the conquest of Kent, and in 838 Archbishop Ceolnoth, in a council held at Kingston, made a treaty of perpetual alliance between his Church and Ecgberht and his son Æthelwulf, the under-king of Kent. By this alliance the Church pledged itself to support the line of kings under which the English at last became a united nation.

The Church
 in relation
 to the State.

No distinct lines divide the area of the Church's work in legislation or jurisdiction from that occupied by the State. Bishops, in virtue of their spiritual dignity, formed part of the witan, first of the several kingdoms, and then of the united nation. In the witenagemóts laws were enacted concerning religion, morality, and ecclesiastical discipline, as well as secular matters; for the clergy had no reason to fear lay interference, and gladly availed themselves of the authority that was attached to the decrees of the national council. The evangelization of the people caused some modification of their ancient laws and customs, and Æthelberht of Kent and other kings published written codes "after the Roman model," in accordance with the teaching of their bishops. It is evident that bishops were usually appointed, and often elected, in the witenagemót. Wilfrith was elected, "by common consent," in a meeting of the Northumbrian witan, and the election of Ealdhelm by the West Saxon assembly is said to have been made by the great men, the clergy, and a multitude of people, though it must not be supposed that the popular voice was ever heard except in assent. Nor does it seem certain that even the form of election was always observed; for, to take a single instance, Ceadda's appointment to Lichfield seems to have been made by Theodore at the request of the Mercian king. The clergy of the bishop's church, however, had a right of election, for Alcuin wrote to the clergy of York reminding them that the election of the archbishop belonged to them. Episcopal elections were, indeed, the results of amicable arrangement, and exemplify the undefined condition of the relations between the Church and the State, and the harmony that existed between them. The Church, however, had its own councils. These were either national, such as that held by Theodore at Hatfield, or, after the restoration of the northern archiepiscopate, provincial, or assemblies of the Church of a single kingdom, such as the Synod of Whitby. In spite of the canon directing that national Church councils should meet annually, they were not often held, owing to the constant strife between the kingdoms. An amendment to one of Theodore's canons proves the freedom of discussion and voting at these assemblies. Provincial councils were attended by a few of the principal clergy of each diocese, who came up to them with their bishop. Kings and nobles were often present at ecclesiastical councils, and joined in attesting their proceedings, so that it is sometimes difficult to decide whether a council was a clerical assembly or a meeting of the witan.

The harmony between Church and State is no less evident in matters of jurisdiction than it is in legislation. Besides exercising jurisdiction in his own franchise, the bishop sat with the ealdorman and sheriff in the local courts, declaring the ecclesiastical law and taking cognizance of the breach of it. Certain cases touching morality appear to have specially belonged to his jurisdiction, which was also exercised in the local courts over criminal clergy. Apart from his work in these courts, he enforced ecclesiastical discipline, and the rules contained in the Penitentials, or codes in which a special penance was provided for each sin. These compilations derived their authority not from any decree, but from their inherent excellence, or from the character of their authors. Some Penitentials were drawn up by Scottish teachers, and Theodore, Bæda, and Ecgberht of York wrote others for the English Church. The bishop had a court of his own for the correction of clergy not accused of civil crime and for the administration of penitential discipline. His chief officer, the archdeacon, first appears under that title, though without territorial jurisdiction, early in the ninth century. Before that time the bishop was attended by his deacon, but this office was one of personal service rather than of administration. No jealousy can be discerned between Church and State, and though the area within which each worked was not clearly defined, it is clear that they worked together without clashing.

The Church
and the
Papacy.

While, however, the Church had this strongly national character, it was in obedience to the Roman see. Archbishops did not consecrate bishops until they had received the pall from the Pope. At first the pall was sent to them, but by the beginning of the eighth century they were expected to fetch it, and this soon became an invariable rule, which strengthened the idea of the dependence of the Church, and afforded opportunities for extortion and aggression. No legates landed here from the time of Theodore until two were sent over by Hadrian in 786. Hadrian's legates held synods in both the two provinces, and published a body of canons, which the kings and their thegns, the archbishops, bishops, and all who attended pledged themselves to obey. By one of these the payment of tithes was, we have seen, made part of the law of the land. Another illustrates the influence of the Church on the conception of kingship. Although the crown invested the king with personal pre-eminence, there was as yet no idea of the sanctity conferred by the religious rite of anointing, which had taken the place of the old Teutonic ceremonies. It was now ordained that no one of illegitimate birth should be chosen king, for none such might enter the priesthood, and that any one who plotted the king's death should be held guilty of the sin of Judas, because the king was the Lord's Anointed. The Church, however, was not to fall into the snare of adulation; bishops were to speak the word of God to kings without fear, and kings were to obey them as those who held the keys of Heaven.

For the next three hundred years the Church was almost wholly free from the direct control of legatine visits. Appeals to the judgment of the Roman see had for the first time been made by Wilfrith, and the Church, as we have seen, cordially upheld the resistance offered by kings and nobles to the Pope's attempts to set aside the decision of national councils. The compromise that was at last effected was not a papal triumph. Nevertheless the authority of the Pope was generally acknowledged, and the most powerful kings thought it needful to obtain the sanction of Rome for ecclesiastical changes, such as the erection and suppression of the Mercian archbishopric. Moreover, Englishmen venerated Rome as the Apostolic See and the mother of Catholic Christendom, and made frequent pilgrimages thither. First, ecclesiastics journeyed to Rome either for purposes of business or devotion. Then, towards the end of the seventh century, Ceadwalla, a West Saxon king, went thither to receive baptism, praying that he might die as soon as he was cleansed from his sins, and his prayer was granted. His example was followed by other kings, and among them by his successor, Ini. Crowds of persons of both sexes and every condition now went on pilgrimage. In Offa's time there were special buildings at Rome called the "Saxon School" for the accommodation of English pilgrims, and the Mercian king obtained a promise from Charles the Great that they should be free of toll in passing through his dominions.

The Church
and Western
Christendom.

The missionary labours of Willibrord, of Winfrith or Boniface, and other Englishmen brought our Church into close relationship with other Churches of Western Europe, for a constant correspondence was kept up between the missionaries and their brethren at home. The connexion between the English and Frankish Churches was strengthened by the residence of Alcuin at the court of Charles the Great, and by the desire of Offa to establish friendly relations with the Frankish monarch. Alcuin obtained a letter from the kings and bishops of England, agreeing with the condemnation which Charles pronounced against the decree of the Second Council of Nice, re-establishing the worship of images in the Eastern Church, and English bishops attended the council Charles held at Frankfort, where the action of the Greeks and the opinions of certain Adoptionist heretics were condemned. At the close of the eighth century our Church was highly esteemed throughout Western Christendom, and this was due both to the noble work accomplished by

English missionaries and to the literary greatness of Northumbria, the home of Alcuin.

———————————————

CHAPTER III.

RUIN AND REVIVAL.

RUIN OF NORTHUMBRIA—
ÆTHELWULF'S PILGRIMAGE—
DANISH INVASIONS OF SOUTHERN
ENGLAND; THE PEACE OF
WEDMORE—ALFRED'S WORK—
CHARACTER OF THE CHURCH IN
THE TENTH CENTURY—
REORGANIZATION—REVIVAL—
ODA—DUNSTAN—SECULARS AND
REGULARS—DUNSTAN'S
ECCLESIASTICAL
ADMINISTRATION—CORONATIONS
—DUNSTAN'S LAST DAYS—
ÆLFRIC THE GRAMMARIAN.

Ruin of
Northumbria.

Before the end of the eighth century the Northmen laid waste Lindisfarne, Jarrow, and Wearmouth. Civil disorder, however, was well nigh as fatal to the Church in the north as the ravages of the heathen. In 808 Archbishop Eanbald joined the Mercian king, Cenwulf, in dethroning Eardulf of Northumbria. Eardulf sought help from the Emperor, Charles the Great, and laid his case before Leo III. A papal legate and an imperial messenger were sent to England to summon Eanbald to appear either before the Pope or the Emperor. He defended himself by letter; his defence was pronounced unsatisfactory, and the Emperor procured the restoration of the king. For the next sixty years anarchy and violence prevailed in the north. Then the Scandinavian pirates invaded the country and overthrew York. Nine years later Halfdene desolated Bernicia, so that not a church was left standing between the Tweed and the Tyne. The bishop of Lindisfarne and his monks fled from their home, carrying with them the bones of St. Cuthberht. They found shelter at Chester-le-Street, which for about a century became the see of the Bernician bishopric. Northumbria became a Danish province, and when it was again brought under the dominion of an English king it had fallen far behind the rest of the country in ecclesiastical and intellectual matters. The Danish conquest had a marked effect upon the position of the northern metropolitan. Cut off from communication with the rest of England, the Northumbrians became almost a distinct nation. The extinction of the native kingship and a long series of revolutions threw political power into the hands of the archbishops, and when the Church of York again emerges from obscurity we find them holding a kind of national headship. Their position was magnified by isolation. While the sees of Hexham and Withern had been overthrown, and the Church of Lindisfarne was in exile, the see of York remained to attract the sympathies and, in more than one instance, direct the action, of the northern people.

During the attacks of the pirates on the south of England the alliance between the Church and the West Saxon throne was strengthened by the common danger, and the bishops appear as patriots and statesmen. Æthelwulf was supported in his struggles with the Danes by Swithun, bishop of Winchester, and Ealhstan, bishop of Sherborne. Ealhstan was rich, and used his wealth for the defence of the kingdom; he equipped armies, joined in leading them in battle, and in 845, in conjunction with the ealdormen of Somerset and Dorset, headed the forces of his bishopric, and inflicted a severe defeat upon the invaders at the mouth of the Parret. The resistance the Danes met with from the West Saxons, which was largely due to the exertions of these bishops, delivered Wessex from invasion for twenty years. Meanwhile Lindsey and East Anglia were ravaged, Canterbury was twice sacked, and London was taken by storm. Everywhere the heathens showed special hatred to the monks and clergy; monasteries and churches were sacked and burnt, and priests were slain with the sword. Æthelwulf's pilgrimage, 855. These calamities were regarded as Divine judgments, and when Æthelwulf had checked the invaders he made a pilgrimage to Rome. Before he left, and after his return, he made a series of donations, which have been described as conveying a tenth part of his own estates to ecclesiastical bodies, and to various thegns, as freeing a tenth part of the folcland from all burdens except the three that fell on all lands alike, and as charging every ten hides of his land with the support of a poor man. Though these grants have nothing to do with the institution of tithes, they illustrate the sacredness that was attached to the tenth portion of property. Æthelwulf carried rich gifts to Benedict III., and while he was at Rome rebuilt the "Saxon School." This institution was supported by a yearly contribution from England, which appears to have been the origin of Peter's pence. The king probably found his youngest son Alfred at Rome, for he had sent him to Leo IV. two years before. Leo confirmed the child, and anointed him as king. The Pope did not, of course, pretend to dispose of the English crown, and probably only meant to consecrate Alfred to any kingship to which his father as head-king might appoint him.

By 870 the whole of the north and east of England had been conquered by the Danes. In that year Eadmund, the East Anglian king, went out to battle against them, and was defeated and taken prisoner. His captors offered to spare his life and restore his kingdom to him, if he would deny Christ and reign under their orders. When he refused their offers, they tied him to a tree, shot at him with arrows, and finally cut off his head. In later days the Abbey of St. Edmund's Bury was named after the martyred king. Wessex well nigh shared the fate of the rest of the country; it was saved by the skill and wisdom of Alfred. Through all the bitter struggle the Church vigorously upheld the national cause; a bishop of Elmham fell fighting against the heathen host in East Anglia, and a bishop of Sherborne in Wessex. Treaty of Wedmore, 878. At last Alfred inflicted a crushing defeat upon the Danish king, Guthorm, at Edington, and as the price of peace Guthorm promised to quit Wessex and accepted Christianity. He was baptized at Wedmore, in Somerset, and a treaty was made by which England was divided into two parts. Wessex was freed from the danger of conquest, and Alfred's immediate dominions were increased, while the north and east remained under the Danes. Guthorm owned the supremacy of the West Saxon king in East Anglia; his people became Christians, and in the other Danish districts the invaders for the most part also accepted Christianity when they became settled in the land.

Alfred's
work.

The Danish wars had a disastrous effect on religion, morality, and learning. The monastic congregations were scattered, and men did not care to become monks. Pure Benedictinism was as yet unknown in England, and a laxer system seems to have prevailed. This system, such as it was, now gave way altogether, and the monasteries that survived the ravages of the Danes fell into the hands of secular clergy, who enjoyed their estates without conforming to any rule, and who were generally married. The collapse of monasticism entailed the decay of learning, for the monastic schools were generally closed. Nor were the parish priests capable of supplying the place of the monks as teachers of the people. The drain of men entailed by the war made it necessary to confer the priesthood on many who were ignorant and otherwise unfit for full orders. And it is probable that the losses which the Church sustained during the war were not confined to monastic bodies, and that the clergy suffered considerably. A general decline in their character and efficiency naturally followed; and Alfred records how England had changed in this respect even within his own memory. He remembered the time when the "sacred orders were zealous in teaching and learning, and in all the services they owed to God, and how foreigners hied to this land for wisdom and lore;" but now, he says, "we should have to get them from abroad." For "there were very few on this side Humber who could understand their rituals in English, or translate a letter from Latin into English, and not many beyond Humber."

There was little difference between the priest and his people; the clergy shared largely in the national habit of excessive drinking, and many priests were married. Among the laity morality was at a low ebb; the marriage tie was lightly regarded, and there was a general return to the laxity and vices of paganism. Heathen customs gathered fresh strength, and women dealt in enchantments and called up ghostly forms. Alfred determined to save his people from barbarism; he set himself to be their teacher, and sought for others to help in his work. From the English part of Mercia, where learning was more advanced than in Wessex, he brought Plegmund, who was afterwards chosen archbishop, and other clerks; Bishop Asser came to him from Wales; from beyond sea, Grimbold, a monk of St. Bertin's, and John from the old Saxon land. He desired that every youth whose parents could afford it should be sent to school till he could read English well, and those who hoped for promotion till they could read Latin. Accordingly, he set up a school for young nobles in his palace, and made education the prominent feature in a monastery he founded at Athelney. He translated into English such books as he thought most needful for his people to read, and probably began the national record called the "Anglo-Saxon Chronicle" in the form we now have it. The care with which he fostered vernacular literature led to the use of English in religious teaching, and to the composition of books of homilies in that language. His code of laws, which consists of a selection from earlier laws and the decrees of synods, contains many ecclesiastical provisions; it treats religion as the foundation of civil law, and begins with the Ten Commandments and an account of the precepts of Moses. As the over-lord of Guthorm, he joined him in publishing a special code for the people of East Anglia, by which apostasy was declared a crime, negligent priests were to be fined, the payment of Peter's pence was commanded, and the practice of heathen rites was forbidden. Alfred brought his kingdom into renewed relations with Rome, for year after year he sent thither alms from himself and his people, probably re-establishing the payment of Peter's pence, which had been interrupted during the period of invasion.

An increased spirit of worldliness in the Church was one of the fruits of the Danish invasions. Alfred endeavoured to check this spirit, and bade his bishops disengage themselves from secular matters and give themselves to wisdom. Nevertheless the very work that he and his immediate successors did for the Church tended to strengthen its connexion with worldly affairs. When it seemed to have lost the power of spontaneous revival, new energy was imparted to it by the action of the Crown. Its revival was in the first instance due to external interference, and this naturally led to the gradual discontinuance of ecclesiastical councils. No decline in influence or activity is implied by this change. Legislation was frequent, but it either took the form of canons put forth by bishops or was part of the work of the witan. The relations between the Church and the State grew closer. Some witenagemóts almost bore the character of Church councils, were largely attended by abbots as well as bishops, and were mainly concerned with ecclesiastical business. During the tenth century the administration of the kingdom was largely carried on by churchmen; and though the statesmen-bishops did not, as at a later period, subordinate their sacred duties to their secular employments, bishoprics came to be regarded in a secular spirit, and plurality was practised. While it is evident that the spiritual jurisdiction of the bishops was in no degree diminished, and, indeed, that it must have gained by the exercise of judicial functions by archdeacons, the clergy, besides being under the bishop's law, were subject to the general police arrangements of the kingdom, and were equally with laymen bound to provide sureties for their orderly behaviour. In every respect the Church had a national character; its development was closely connected with the national progress; its bishops were national officers; its laws were decreed in the national assembly, and it was free from papal interference; for throughout the tenth century no appeals were carried to Rome, and no legate appears to have set foot in the country.

Reorganization.

Several changes took place in the episcopate of the southern province during the period of invasion. Dunwich ceased to have a bishop, and Elmham, though the succession there was broken, became the only East Anglian see. Little more is heard of the bishopric of Lindsey, and the bishop of Leicester moved his see to the Oxfordshire Dorchester, so as to be within reach of West Saxon help. On the other hand, the renewed energy of the Church in Wessex led to an extension of the episcopate south of the Thames. In 909 the sees of Winchester, Sherborne, and South Saxon Selsey all happened to be vacant, and, according to a story that must certainly be rejected as it stands, Pope

Formosus, who was then dead, reproached King Eadward the Elder for his neglect in the matter. Eadward had a good adviser in Archbishop Plegmund; with the consent of his witan, he separated Wiltshire and Berkshire from the see of Winchester, and formed them into the new diocese of Ramsbury, and further created two other new bishoprics for Somerset and Devon, placing the sees at Wells and Crediton. Five West Saxon bishops, together with two for Selsey and Dorchester, were, it is said, consecrated at once. The extension of the power of the English king brought with it an extension of the power of the Church. South Wales owned the supremacy of Alfred, and accordingly South Welsh bishops received consecration at Canterbury and professed obedience to Archbishop Æthelred. Eadward's victories in East Anglia were followed by the republication of the laws of Alfred and Guthorm, and the diocesan system appears to have been gradually restored in Mercia. Eadward's son, Æthelstan, annexed Cornwall, the land of the West Welsh, and this addition to the English kingdom was added to the province of Canterbury; for Cornwall was made an English diocese, and its see was placed at St. German's, or Bodmin. Lastly, the conquest of Northumbria by Æthelstan, who put the Danish prince Guthred to flight and took possession of York, is marked ecclesiastically by his appointment of Wulfstan to the archbishopric. Throughout Æthelstan's reign the influence of churchmen is clearly apparent. His ecclesiastical laws, enacted along with others on secular matters in a witenagemót at Greatley, near Andover, for the Mercian shires, and republished elsewhere for other parts of the kingdom, were made by the advice of Archbishop Wulfhelm and other bishops. Tithes both of animals and fruits were to be paid from the king's lands, and his reeves and ealdormen were bidden to charge those subject to them to make like payments: the part of the Church in secular jurisdiction was confirmed by the regulation of ordeals by the hallowed bread (or "housel"), by water, and by hot iron, and fresh enactments were made against heathen practices.

Ecclesiastical
revival.

Although Alfred and his immediate successors did much for the Church, especially as regards its external position, the ecclesiastical revival that distinguished the latter part of the century was primarily effected by means of a monastic reformation. This reformation was necessary for the salvation of society; for as long as monks and nuns remained unworthy of their vocation, the simple priest could never have been brought to live as he was bound to do; and as long as his life was no higher or purer than the lives of his flock, there was no means of elevating the people. While most of those who were foremost in the work of revival were of purely English descent, the bracing influence of the Danish colonization extended to the area of ecclesiastical as well as of civil life. As soon as a Dane was converted he became a member of the English Church, and the Church thus became a powerful instrument in promoting the amalgamation of the two peoples. She reaped her reward in gaining the services of the Danish Oda and his nephew Oswald. At the same time, the reformers of this age, though aided in their work by the Crown, would not have attained their measure of success had it not been for the teaching and encouragement they received from abroad. This connexion between our Church and the monasteries of the Continent was largely due to the foreign alliances formed by the house of Ecgberht. Of late years Alfred had given one of his daughters in marriage to a count of Flanders, and Æthelstan had married his sisters to Otto of Germany, to Charles, the king of the West Franks, and other princes. Accordingly, the monasteries of Northern France and Flanders became the patterns by which our reformers worked; their congregations took deep interest in the affairs of our Church, received liberal aid from England, and held our noblest churchmen in high esteem.

Archbishop
Oda, 942-
959.

Oda, the son of one of the fierce band of Ivar, was converted to Christianity in early life, and was in consequence driven from his father's house. He entered the household of an English thegn, who had him taught Latin, and, it is said, Greek also, persuaded him to be ordained, and took him to Rome. He became one of King Eadward's clerks, and Æthelstan made him bishop of Ramsbury and employed him in affairs of state. In 937 Oda, in company with two other bishops, was present at the battle of Brunanburh, and did the king good service either by miraculously obtaining a new sword for him when he had broken his own, or by handing him a weapon as another warrior might have done. Eadmund, who, like his brother Æthelstan, chose his ministers among ecclesiastics, offered him the archbishopric of Canterbury. Like his successor, Thomas, in later days, Oda was by nature a statesman and a soldier rather than a priest, but, like him, he determined when he accepted the primacy to act up to the highest standard of ecclesiastical life. He declared that no one ought to be archbishop who was not a monk, and accordingly received the monastic habit from the famous abbey of Fleury. As archbishop, he sought to bring about a reformation of morals. In a pastoral letter he urged all spiritual persons to purity of life; he insisted on the sanctity of marriage, and in a witenagemót held at London in 944 took part in making laws providing for the protection, maintenance, and dower of wives, and ordering that all marriages should be solemnized by a priest, and that care should be taken that there was no bar of consanguinity. He probably found an efficient ally in Ælfheah, or Elphege, the Bald, bishop of Winchester, who appears to have laboured to bring about a faithful discharge of monastic vows.

Dunstan.

The work of Oda is overshadowed by that of Dunstan, the kinsman and disciple of Bishop Ælfheah. Dunstan was a West Saxon, and was brought up partly at Glastonbury and partly at the court of Æthelstan, for he was connected with the royal house. With a highly strung and imaginative nature he combined much practical wisdom and determination of character. Full of piety, skilled in music and the other arts, a cunning craftsman, and endued with the power of winning the love and influencing the conduct of others, he was at an early age one of the counsellors of Eadmund. When he was about twenty-one the king made him abbot of Glastonbury. The abbey had fallen into decay, and he at once began to restore and reform it, though not on the Benedictine model. During the reign of Eadred he held the office of royal treasurer. The king was sickly, and the work of government was carried on mainly by Dunstan and the queen-mother. Eadred wished him to accept a bishopric, but he refused, for he would not leave the king's service, and he evidently considered that a bishopric should not be treated as a mere provision for an officer of state. As the king's chief minister, he must have been largely concerned in the reduction of the north, and it may be inferred, from the policy pursued with regard to the archbishop of York, that he was by no means an asserter of clerical immunity. Archbishop Wulfstan had been foremost in the revolt of Northumbria from the West Saxon king. At last Eadred caught him and put him in prison; and though, after a while, he was released and again acted as bishop, he was not allowed to return to his province.

His
banishment,
956.

Soon after the accession of Eadwig, in 956, Dunstan incurred the wrath of a powerful enemy. At his consecration feast the boy-king left the hall for the society of a young lady named Ælfgifu and her mother, Æthelgifu, who wished to make a match between him and her daughter. The great men were wroth at this slight on themselves and on the kingly office, and sent Dunstan to bring Eadwig back to the hall. Now there was some connexion between Eadwig and Ælfgifu that would have made their marriage unlawful, and when Dunstan saw them together his zeal for purity was aroused; hot words passed between him and the girl's mother, and he forced the king to return to the banquet. In revenge Æthelgifu procured his banishment. He found shelter in the abbey of St. Peter at Ghent, where for the first time he saw the rule of St. Benedict fully carried out. While he was there, the people of the north revolted from Eadwig, and chose his younger brother Eadgar as king. Oda took advantage of this revolt to separate Eadwig from Ælfgifu, whom he had

34

by this time married, and it is said that either she or her mother—the story is late and uncertain—was cruelly slain by the insurgents. This revolt of England north of the Thames and the division of the kingdom have little or no ecclesiastical significance, for Oda continued Eadwig's subject until his death. Eadgar, the "king of the Mercians," called Dunstan back to England, and he was raised to the episcopate. The circumstances of his elevation illustrate the unsettled state of the custom as regards episcopal elections. Although no see was vacant, the witan decreed that he should be made bishop, and he appears to have been consecrated accordingly. _{Dunstan archbishop, 960-988.}Shortly afterwards the bishop of Worcester died, and Dunstan was appointed his successor. A few months later he received the bishopric of London, which he held along with Worcester. In 959 Eadwig died, and Eadgar became king south of the Thames. Then Brithelm, bishop of Wells, who had been appointed archbishop by Eadwig, was sent back to his old diocese, and by the counsel of the witan Dunstan was chosen archbishop in his stead.

Seculars
and
regulars.

During the reign of Eadgar the secular clergy were driven out of many of the monasteries south of the Humber, and their places were taken by monks who lived according to the rule of St. Benedict. The chief movers in this change were Æthelwold, who, at Dunstan's request, was made bishop of Winchester; Oswald, bishop of Worcester, who had been a monk of Fleury, and had learnt the Benedictine rule there; and the king himself. Dunstan, though he approved of the movement, did not take any active part in it, and did not disturb the secular canons of his own church. Pope John XIII. wrote to Eadgar, expressing his pleasure at his zeal and authorising the proceedings of Æthelwold. In the north no such change was made, and though Oswald was elected archbishop of York in 972, he did not attempt to turn out the clerks there. While the seculars who were expelled from the monastic churches were, as a rule, married men, no general persecution of the married clergy took place. It was unlawful for a man in the higher orders to marry, and if a married man took these orders, he was bound to put away his wife. But the marriage of the clergy prevailed too widely to be attacked with vigour or success, and though celibacy was the rule of the Church, no effectual measures were taken to enforce it. The only penalty pronounced against the married priest in the canons for which Dunstan is responsible is, that he should lose the privilege of his order; he ceased to be of "thegn-right worthy," and had no higher legal status than that of a layman of equal birth.

Dunstan's
ecclesiastical
administration.

35

The general character of Dunstan's ecclesiastical administration may be gathered from the laws and canons of Eadgar's reign. The laws mark a step in the history of tithes, for they contain the first provision for enforcing payment by legal process, by the joint action of civil and ecclesiastical officers, and they declare the right of the parish priest in certain cases to a portion of the payment made by the landowner, independently of any distribution by the bishop. When a thegn had on his estate of inheritance a church with a burying-ground, it was ordered that he should give one-third to the priest; if his church had no burying-ground, he might give the priest what he pleased. The payment of Peter's pence is also commanded. It is evident from the canons that Dunstan endeavoured to make the clergy the educators of the people; priests were to teach each his own scholars, and not take away the scholars of others; they were to learn handicrafts and instruct their people in them, and to preach a sermon every Sunday. The laity were to avoid concubinage and practise lawful marriage. And both in continence, and in every other respect, the necessity of raising the clergy to a higher level of life than that of the society round them was fully recognized; they were not to hunt, hawk, play at dice, or engage in drinking-bouts, and greater attention was to be paid to ritual, especially in celebrating the Eucharist. While they were thus to be brought, as regards both their lives and the performance of their duties, to a deeper sense of the dignity of their calling, they were socially to hold a high place; a priest engaged in a suit with a thegn was not to be called on to make oath until the thegn had first sworn, and the quarrels of priests were to be decided by a bishop, and not taken before a secular judge. In these and other efforts to raise the character and position of the clergy Dunstan did not desire to make the Church less national, or to separate her ministers from the life of the nation and subject them to the authority of Rome. He worked, as the spiritual ruler of the national Church, for the good both of the Church and the nation, and evidently maintained an independent attitude towards the Pope. A noble, whom he had excommunicated for contracting an unlawful marriage, obtained a papal mandate ordering the archbishop to absolve him. Dunstan flatly refused to obey the order, declaring that he would rather suffer death than be unfaithful to his Lord.

Coronations.

As Eadgar's chief minister, Dunstan must have had a large share in establishing the order and good government that form the special glories of the reign, and the wise policy of non-interference that secured the loyalty of the Danish districts was probably due as much to him as to the king. Cnut seems to have recognized what he had done to make the Danish population part of the English people, for he ordered that St. Dunstan's mass-day should be kept by all as a solemn feast. Dunstan saw the fruit of his political labours.

It has been asserted that Eadgar's coronation at Bath was connected with a penance laid upon him by the archbishop. While it is not improbable that Dunstan imposed a penance on the king for one of the sins of his youth, the story that he forbade him to wear his crown for seven years is mere legend. The coronation at Bath, which was performed by both archbishops, with all the bishops assisting, was the solemn declaration that all the peoples of England were at last united under one sovereign. On Eadgar's death a dispute arose as to the succession. Civil war was on the point of breaking out between the rival ealdormen of East Anglia and Mercia; the Mercian ealdorman turned the monks out of the monasteries and brought the seculars back, while the East Anglian house, which had ever been allied with Dunstan, and had forwarded the monastic policy of Eadgar, took up the cause of the monks. In this crisis the two archbishops preserved the peace of the kingdom; for they declared for Eadward, the elder son of Eadgar, and placed the crown on his head. His short reign was filled with the strife between the seculars and regulars. After his murder the two archbishops joined in crowning Æthelred. Although the increase in the personal power and dignity of the king that marked the age is to some extent to be connected with the teaching of the Church concerning the sanctity of his person and the duty of obedience, still the Church did not favour absolutism. Indeed, in the rite of coronation, which seems to have been brought into special prominence during this period, the king bound himself by an oath to govern well, to defend the Church and all Christian people, to forbid robbery and unrighteous doings to all orders, and to enjoin justice and mercy in all judgments. At Æthelred's coronation Dunstan, after administering this oath, set forth in solemn terms the responsibilities of a "hallowed" king.

Dunstan's
last days.

Dunstan's pre-eminent position in the State magnified the political importance of his see. In his time Kent and Sussex ceased to be ruled by their own ealdormen, and these shires, together with Surrey, were ruled by the archbishop with the authority of an ealdorman. With the accession of Æthelred, Dunstan's influence in the State seems to have ended. During the early years of his reign the king was led by unworthy favourites to seize on some of the possessions of the Church, and among them on some lands of the see of Rochester. The see was in a special manner dependent on Canterbury, and the archbishop may almost be said to have been the lord of the bishopric, an arrangement that evidently sprang from the early dependence of the people of West Kent on the king of the Eastern people. Dunstan threatened to excommunicate the king. Æthelred, however, paid no heed to his threats, and sent his troops to ravage the lands of the see until the archbishop was forced to bribe him to recall them from the siege of Rochester.

Although he was no longer engaged in political matters, Dunstan's last days were not idly spent. As a ruler and judge he was diligent and able. He took much delight in the services of the Church. He corrected and illuminated manuscripts, and practised the crafts in which he excelled, and all who came to him for knowledge found him a patient and gentle teacher. On Ascension Day 988, two days before his death, he celebrated the Holy Mysteries and preached three times. Then he fell sick, and on the following Saturday, after commending his soul to the prayers of the monks of his house, he received the Sacrament, and when he had done so he gave thanks to God and sang, "The merciful and gracious Lord hath so done His marvellous acts that they ought to be had in remembrance. He hath given meat unto them that fear Him"— and with these words he fell asleep.

Ælfric the
Grammarian.

Alfred's attempt to revive learning had met with little success, for no priest, we are told, wrote or understood Latin before the days of Æthelwold and Dunstan. Now, however, along with the rule of St. Benedict, the monastic reformers brought into England the learning of the Benedictine houses of the Continent, and famous schools were established at Winchester, Ramsey, and other monasteries. Nor was the work of teaching confined to the monks; for all parish priests were also schoolmasters, and though few of them had much learning, what they taught was enough to show a boy what he could do; and if he wanted to learn more, he would seek admission into some monastic school. Alfred had taught men that the education of the people should be carried on in their own tongue, and this lesson was learnt and enforced by Ælfric, abbot first of Cerne about 1005, and later of Ensham. Ælfric took much interest in education, and among his other works compiled a Grammar, which he dedicated to the boys of England, and from which he is generally called the "Grammarian." He saw that the people needed religious teaching, and he therefore abridged and translated some of the books of the Old Testament, and compiled two books of homilies, in which, as he says, he used "no obscure words, but plain English, that might come to the hearts of readers and hearers to their souls' good." These homilies and some of his other writings, which must be held to express the doctrines of the English Church in his day and on to the time of the Norman Conquest, differ in some respects from the teaching of the Church of Rome. They contain many declarations against transubstantiation. "The holy housel," Ælfric writes, "is by nature corruptible bread and wine, and is by the power of the divine word truly Christ's body and blood; not, however, bodily but spiritually." He does not give St. Peter the pre-eminence among the apostles that is ascribed to him by Rome, and he refuses to recognize bishops as a distinct order in the Church. He wrote canons for the bishop of Sherborne, and a kind of charge for the archbishop of York. These direct that, according to the ancient custom, tithes should be divided between the repair of the church, the poor, and the parish priest; and they also show that, while priests were strongly urged to put away their wives, no means were taken to compel them to do so. The renewed vigour imparted to the Church by the monastic revival was further manifested by a fresh outburst of missionary zeal; and Sigeferth of York and other priests went forth to preach the Gospel in Norway and Sweden.

CHAPTER IV.

EXHAUSTION.

Characteristics
of the
period, 980-
1066.

From the renewal of the Danish invasions to the conquest of England by the Normans the Church threw itself unreservedly into the affairs of the State, and almost lost all separate life. While churchmen directed the councils of the nation, the conciliar action of the Church ceased altogether. Bishops took a leading part in politics, and the ablest of the clergy were employed in secular administration. The Church did the nation good service during the period of invasion, and finally converted a savage conqueror into a beneficent king. Nevertheless it became worldly, and though it exercised vast power, its own life dwindled and sank with the life of the nation to a lower level. The close union between the Church and the nation strongly affected the history of both alike. The struggle against the foreigners who were promoted by Eadward the Confessor to offices both in Church and State has a strongly marked ecclesiastical side. Foreign bishops brought the Church into new relations with the papacy, and impaired its independence and national character. Still, its close connexion with the State was preserved, and the foreign element which had been imported into it was for a time forcibly crushed by the national party in the kingdom. In the hope of bringing the Church into subjection, Rome blessed the invasion of England, and Church and State alike were prostrated at the feet of the Conqueror. Yet the English Church survived the Conquest, and became a powerful agent in preserving the national life, which before long made the conquerors and the conquered one people.

Renewed
Scandinavian
invasions.

Dunstan's retirement was soon followed by renewed Scandinavian invasions. After his death he was succeeded at Canterbury by Sigeric, who in 991 took a prominent part in purchasing peace from the Norwegian host. Although this was the beginning of a fatal policy, his action, taken by itself, seems capable of defence. It was a moment of pressing danger, and there was no force ready to meet the invader. Sigeric probably hoped that if the Norwegian fleet received payment it would defend the land from other piratical attacks. The invaders of England found shelter in the harbours of Normandy, and this led to a dispute between Æthelred and the Norman duke. War was prevented by the intervention of the Pope, the proper mediator between Christian princes. John XV. sent an envoy to England, and at his request a treaty was made between the king and the duke. Unfortunately, the peace with the Norwegians was broken. A fleet was fitted out for the defence of the coast; two bishops and two lay nobles were entrusted with the command, and, in spite of treachery, it gained one of the few successes of the reign. Two years later an invasion was made by the combined forces of Olaf of Norway, who, it is said, had already received Christianity from English missionaries, and of Swend, the apostate king of Denmark. After a time, Ælfheah (St. Alphege), bishop of Winchester, was sent to treat for peace with Olaf, who was with his fleet at Southampton. The king listened to the bishop's exhortations, and fully accepted the faith into which he had been baptized. He met Æthelred at Andover, and there received confirmation, and promised never to return to England as an enemy. He kept his word, sailed away to evangelize his own dominions, and became one of the most heroic figures in early Scandinavian history. This bloodless victory won by the Church gave the land rest for three years, during which the Bernician see at last found an abiding-place. Fear of the Northmen drove Bishop Ealdhun and his monks to flee from Chester-le-Street. Taking the body of their patron with them, they sought shelter at Ripon, and in 995, when the immediate danger had passed, settled at Durham. There Ealdhun raised his church on the height above the Wear, in that strong place that has had so great an influence on the history of the see. Even in his time the bishopric began to assume its special character as a march against the

Scots.

On Ælfric's death Ælfheah was translated to Canterbury. The new archbishop appears to have laboured to bring about a national reformation. Two meetings of the witan were held, in which the ecclesiastical element was evidently strong. During one of these the bishops and abbots met each day for prayer and consultation, arranging probably the part they would take in the discussions of the assembly. Decrees were made enjoining acts of penitence and the observance of the day of the new saint, Eadward the Martyr. All were to live righteously, were to love one God, uphold one Christendom, and be true to one lord, the king. Measures were also taken for the defence of the kingdom. Thus even a strictly ecclesiastical matter like the observance of a "mass-day" was made a subject of legislation by the national Council. At the same time the assembly was largely ecclesiastical in character, and in its efforts after better things, whether with regard to national unity and defence, or repentance and faith towards God, seems to have followed the guidance of the rulers of the Church.

Efforts such as this, however, were rendered of no avail by the folly of the king, the treachery of the nobles, and the disorganization of the country. In 1011 Thurkill, who was then in command of a Danish fleet, was promised a large sum of money if he would cease from his ravages. Payment was delayed, and the Danes attacked Canterbury, sacked the city, burned the cathedral, and carried off many captives, and among them the archbishop. For seven months they kept Ælfheah in their ships in chains, hunger, and misery. At first he promised to ransom himself; but he repented of this, for he thought of the sufferings of the people from whom the money must be raised. While in captivity he spoke of Christ to those who guarded him, and his words did not fall to the ground. The fleet lay at Greenwich, and no money came either as tribute or for the ransom of the archbishop. On 19th May 1012, the day on which the ransom was due, the Danes made a feast, and drank deeply of some wine they had brought from southern lands. Then they brought the archbishop forth and demanded the ransom. He replied that he would pay nothing, that he was ready to suffer, and that he commended his soul to God. Thurkill saw his danger, and tried to save him, offering all he possessed, except his ship, for his life. But they would not hearken, and pelted Ælfheah with stones and the bones of the oxen which they had eaten, until at last one who had been converted by the archbishop, and whom he had confirmed the day before, put him out of his agony by cleaving his head with his battle-axe. Ælfheah did not die in vain. Soon after his martyrdom Thurkill, whom we may believe he had converted, declared himself a Christian, and brought his ships and their crews to serve the English king. Ælfheah laid down his life for the sake of the poor, and his death gave England an ally who, during the remainder of Æthelred's reign, defended her to the utmost of his power against the attacks of his own countrymen.

End of the
Danish war.

At last Æthelred was forced to flee from his kingdom, and Swend was chosen king. His reign was short. He had a special hatred for the memory of Eadmund, the martyred king of East Anglia, and threatened to destroy his church and put its priests to death by torture. As he was on his way thither he was struck by death, and men said that he cried out that the armed figure of the martyred king appeared to him and smote him with his weapon. Æthelred returned to his kingdom after Swend's death, and soon after his return held a witenagemót, by the advice of Archbishop Lyfing. In the decrees of this assembly the influence of the Church is again strongly marked; they are mainly expressions of desires for national repentance, reformation, and unity. One resolution is especially noteworthy. It seems as if some assemblies had been held which had treated of secular, or perhaps of ecclesiastical, matters exclusively. This was declared to be wrong; Christ's law and the king's law were to be declared together, as in old time. In the struggle between Eadmund and Cnut, which soon followed, churchmen gave their lives for the national cause; for after Eadmund's last battle at Assandun the bishop of Dorchester and other clergy were found among the slain. Some late writers say that they came to pray, and not to fight.

Cnut and
the Church,
1017-1035.

In the change that came over the character of Cnut, soon after he ascended the throne, we may discern that the Church won a spiritual victory of much the same kind as the conversions of Olaf and Thurkill. The fierce barbarian became a wise and just ruler. This change was, it may be gathered, largely due to the influence of Æthelnoth, called the Good, whom Cnut made archbishop after the death of Lyfing. Cnut's ecclesiastical laws consist mainly of repetitions from earlier codes: the "mass-days" of King Eadward and Archbishop Dunstan were to be observed by all, men were to go to "housel" three times a year at least, and the clergy were to instruct their flocks diligently. One law declares the liability of the laity to maintain churches —"all people ought of right to help to repair the church." Cnut gave largely to monasteries, and, moreover, built at Assandun, in commemoration of his victory, a secular, or non-monastic, church which was served by a priest named Stigand. He made a pilgrimage to Rome in 1026-7, and while he was there wrote a letter addressed to the two archbishops and all the English people, telling them how honourably he had been received by the Pope and the Emperor Conrad; how he had spoken to them of the wants of his people, and Conrad had promised that the merchants and pilgrims of England and Denmark should not be oppressed with tolls when they crossed the Alps. To the Pope he said that he was much annoyed to find that his archbishops had to pay vast sums when they fetched their palls, and it was decreed that this should be so no longer. He told his people how anxious he was to rule well, and, among other matters, charged the bishops and reeves to see that all tithes, Peter's pence, and church dues were paid up by the time he came back.

This letter was addressed to the archbishops by name, for they were, in virtue of their office, the recognized heads of the people of England. The authority of the archbishop of Canterbury was, no doubt, strengthened by the influence that Æthelnoth exercised over the king. Its extent is illustrated by the story that after Cnut's death Æthelnoth refused to crown Harold, declaring that the sons of Emma had a prior claim. Although this story may not be true, it at least shows that it was held not to be impossible that the archbishop should have acted thus. The see of Canterbury gained special splendour from Cnut's policy with regard to the different kingdoms under his dominion. He treated England as the head of his northern empire, and carried this policy out in ecclesiastical as well as in civil matters; for he appointed certain English priests to Danish sees, and caused Æthelnoth to consecrate them. They must, therefore, have professed obedience to Canterbury. This roused the anger of the archbishop of Hamburg, the metropolitan of the North, and Cnut promised that it should not happen again.

The king's
clerks.

Although the archbishop of Canterbury, and indeed the bishops generally, had considerable political influence at this period, Cnut's chief minister was a layman, and this had an important bearing on the progress of a change in the administrative machinery of the kingdom that deeply affected the Church. As long as the chief minister of the king was an ecclesiastic, the clergy who carried on the routine of government under his direction naturally had no distinct position. Now, however, the king's clerks or chaplains begin to appear as a recognized body of officials discharging the ordinary business of the administration. When Cnut visited different parts of the kingdom he took four of these clerks with him; for his journeys were really judicial circuits, and he needed clerks to register his decrees and other acts. Deeds and charters drawn up by these clerical secretaries were, when necessary, kept in the royal chapel, of which they were the priests. In the Confessor's reign it became customary for the king to signify his will by sealed writs, and an officer was appointed to keep the king's seal. He was called the chancellor, from the screen (*cancelli*) behind which the secretaries worked. He was chief of the royal clerks, and the institution of his office gave further distinctness to the body over which he presided. The king's clerks were generally rewarded with bishoprics or other ecclesiastical preferments; and thus, while the State gained the services of a body of trained officials, the Church lost much; Spiritual decadence.for the surest path to preferment lay in the discharge of secular rather than of religious duties, and many of its chief ministers were servants of an earthly rather than of a Heavenly King. Indeed, from the death of Cnut to the Norman Conquest, the life of the Church is marked by increasing worldliness. Bishops played a large part in the affairs of the nation, but, for the most part, had little regard for their spiritual duties. Bishoprics were sought after as sources of wealth and power, and were often obtained by simony and held in plurality. While Wulfstan of Worcester was a man of holy life, Leofric of Exeter an ecclesiastical reformer, and Ealdred of York a prelate of conspicuous energy, most of the bishops of this period were simply greedy, second-rate men. Nor do the inferior clergy appear to have been better than their rulers; for baptism is said to have been much neglected, because the clergy refused to administer it without a fee.

Eadward
the
Confessor,
1042-1066.

On the death of Harthacnut, in 1042, the line of Danish kings ended, and Eadward the Confessor, a representative of the old English royal house, was chosen king, mainly through the influence of Earl Godwine. In spite of his saintly reputation, Eadward did no good to the Church; for he did not strive to appoint faithful bishops. He might have done so; for, though the clergy had a right of election, and appointments were made in the witenagemót, the king certainly at this time generally gave bishoprics to whom he would. It rested with him to issue the writ for consecration, and he invested the new prelate with the temporalities of the see by the gift of the ring and staff. Eadward, even if guiltless of simony himself, took no pains to ensure the purity of episcopal appointments, and treated them simply as a means of gratifying his favourites. His long residence in Normandy had made him more of a Frenchman than an Englishman. Foreigners appointed to English sees.He loved to have foreigners about him, and promoted Normans to English bishoprics without any regard for their fitness, giving London to Robert of Jumièges, a meddlesome politician, who had unbounded influence with him, and setting Ulf, one of his Norman clerks, who was grossly ignorant of ecclesiastical things, over the diocese of Dorchester. The Norman party of the court was opposed by Earl Godwine, the king's chief minister, and it is probable that the appointment of certain Lotharingians to English sees was due to his desire to counterbalance the influence of the Norman bishops. That even Godwine, the head of the national party, should, in the hope of strengthening his position, have procured English bishoprics for foreigners seems to prove that native churchmen of learning and high character were scarce.

Effect of
  these
appointments.

All the foreign bishops, Normans and Lotharingians alike, were accustomed to greater dependence on Rome than had ever been owned in England, and the effect of their appointment was to weaken the national character of the Church. We now for the first time find bishops, after they had been nominated by the king, going to Rome for confirmation, and the Roman court claiming to have the right to reject a royal nomination. Various matters, too, were now referred to the Pope for decision, contrary to the custom of the English Church. Other foreign fashions were also introduced. In England, any place was chosen for a bishop's see that was a convenient centre for diocesan work; on the Continent, bishops always had their sees in cities. Leofric, bishop of Crediton, a Lotharingian by education though not by birth, naturally had foreign ideas, and wished to transfer his see from the village of Crediton to the city of Exeter. He did not first apply to the king for leave to make this change, as any of his predecessors would have done, but asked Pope Leo IX. for his sanction. Leo wrote to Eadward expressing his surprise that Leofric should have "a see without a city," and requesting that the change should be made. At the same time, the removal was actually effected in virtue of a charter granted by the king in 1050 with the consent of the witan. When, after the Conquest, foreigners were dominant in the Church, the translation of sees from villages to cities was, as we shall see, widely carried out. Leofric also made the clergy of his cathedral conform to a rule observed by canons in Lotharingia, called the rule of Chrodegang of Metz; he would not allow them to live in their own houses, and forced them to sleep in a common dormitory and eat at a common table. This gave his chapter a character that was half monastic and half secular, and, of course, prevented the clergy from living as married men. The system was introduced at Wells by the Lotharingian bishop Gisa, and, with some modifications, at York by Ealdred; but it never took root in England. The influence of the foreign prelates may also be traced in the presence of English bishops at papal councils. Several attended the council

46

which Leo held at Rheims in 1049, and also his council at Vercelli the next year. At Vercelli, Ulf sought the papal confirmation of his appointment to the bishopric of Dorchester, and, we are told, "they were very nigh breaking his staff," because he could not perform the Service of the Church. Nevertheless, ignorant as he was, he was allowed to keep his office; for he spent a large sum in bribery.

Party
struggles.

In 1050 a trial of strength took place between the national and foreign parties at the court with reference to an election to the see of Canterbury. The monks of Christ Church chose one of their number, named Ælfric, a kinsman of Earl Godwine, and their choice was approved by the clergy. Godwine begged the king to accept Ælfric, but he refused, and appointed his Norman favourite, Robert of Jumièges, to the primacy, and Spearhafoc, abbot of Abingdon, an Englishman and a skilful goldsmith, who was making a crown for him, to the bishopric of London. When Robert came back from Rome with his pall he refused to obey the king's order that he should consecrate Spearhafoc, declaring that the Pope had forbidden him to do so. Spearhafoc, however, though he was not consecrated, kept the bishopric for some months. Archbishop Robert succeeded in undermining Godwine's influence with the king, and a quarrel became imminent. Some attempt at mediation was made by Stigand, bishop of Winchester, originally the priest of Cnut's church at Assandun, who had been appointed by Harthacnut to the see of Elmham. He lost this see because some one offered the king money for it, and regained it probably by giving a larger sum. He was not consecrated until 1043; then he was deprived by Eadward for political reasons, but made his peace with the king, and again regained his bishopric. He belonged to Godwine's party, and was translated to Winchester while the earl was in power. His attempt at mediation failed; Godwine and his sons were outlawed by the witan, and the foreigners became dominant in Church and State. Spearhafoc was now ousted, and the bishopric of London was given to one of the king's Norman clerks, named William. The next year Godwine anchored at Southwark with an armed force. When the Frenchmen found that his restoration was certain they fled. Robert and Ulf cut their way through the streets of London, and the archbishop "betook himself over sea, and left his pall and all Christendom here on land, so as God willed it, as he had before gotten his worship as God willed it not." He and all his countrymen were outlawed, and Stigand was appointed archbishop in his stead. William of London was, however, allowed to return to his see, because he had made himself acceptable to the people.

Earl Harold.

The English clergy generally were on the side of Godwine, as the champion of the national cause; and when his son Harold succeeded to his earldom and power, they seem to have upheld him also. Harold was a more religious man than his father, who was greedy and unscrupulous, and laid hands on some of the possessions of the Church. Unlike the other chief nobles of England at this time, Godwine was not a benefactor to any religious house. His son, however, founded a church at Waltham in honour of the Holy Rood. Contrary to the fashion of the day, he made his foundation collegiate, not monastic; he did not build his church for monks, whose special aim was to secure their own salvation, but made it a college of secular clergy or canons, whose duty it was to do good to others. He intended his college to be a place of education; for the chancellor of the church was to deliver lectures, and, as learning was scarce in England, he gave the office of chancellor to a foreigner, Adelard of Liége. Two Lotharingians were appointed to bishoprics after Harold became the king's chief minister, so that in this respect he seems to have followed the ecclesiastical policy of his father.

In addition to the Romanizing influence exercised on the Church during this reign by foreign prelates, the revival of the custom of making pilgrimages, due perhaps to the example of Cnut, perhaps to increased communication with the Normans, with whom this form of devotion was exceedingly popular, tended to magnify the papal authority in England. Eadward himself vowed to go on pilgrimage to Rome. The witan, however, told him that he ought not to leave the country, and, it is said, advised him to pray the Pope to remit his vow. At all events he sent Ealdred, then bishop of Worcester, and the bishop of Ramsbury for that purpose to Rome. Leo granted the king's request, and by his direction Eadward built Westminster Abbey instead of making the pilgrimage. Harold and his brothers, Tostig and Gyrth, all visited Rome. Tostig was accompanied by Ealdred, who in 1061 went to fetch his pall after he had received the see of York. Ealdred was a notable pluralist; he had administered three dioceses at once, and was now holding the diocese of Worcester, which he intended to keep along with York, as had been the custom almost ever since Oswald's time. Nicolas II. refused to grant him the pall, accused him of ignorance, simony, and plurality, and of having accepted translation without his permission, and actually declared him degraded from the episcopal order. As he and Tostig were on their way home they were robbed by brigands at Sutri. This was lucky for Ealdred. They returned to Rome, and the fierce earl rated the Pope soundly. If this, he said, was the treatment English pilgrims were to expect, he would find that he would get no more money from England; the king should be told of the whole affair. The Pope was frightened; he was reconciled to Ealdred, and granted him the pall on his agreeing to give up Worcester. Besides those who journeyed to Rome, some English people went on pilgrimage to Jerusalem, and among them Ealdred, before he was made archbishop, had journeyed thither, "with such worshipfulness as none had ever shown before."

Soon after Ealdred returned from Rome with his pall two legates landed in England. This was an unusual event, for the Church had been virtually free from legatine interference for nearly three centuries, and this visit marks the change that had been effected in her relations with the Papacy during the reign of Eadward. By the advice of these legates, Wulfstan was chosen bishop of Worcester by the "clergy and people" of the city, and his election was approved by the witan. No better choice could have been made.

49

Although the independence of the Church had been impaired, its national character was still strong. No better proof can be given of this than the ecclesiastical changes consequent on Earl Godwine's return. Robert and Ulf were deprived of their sees simply by a decree of the witan, and Stigand received the archbishopric as a reward for political services. As far as regards character, he was certainly no better fitted for the office than his Norman predecessor; for he was worldly and grasping, and retained the see of Winchester along with the archbishopric. It was obvious that as long as Robert lived no one could canonically hold his office; and though Stigand enjoyed the revenues of Canterbury, he was not looked on as a canonical archbishop, and he had not received the pall. Robert carried his wrongs to Rome, and his deprivation was pronounced unlawful; so Stigand could not hope that the pall would be granted him. For some years he wore the pall which Robert left behind him, but bishops-elect would not receive consecration at his hands; at last he obtained a pall from Benedict X. As, however, Benedict failed to make his position good, and was reckoned an anti-pope, Stigand was involved in the guilt of his schism. Indeed, though the gift of this pall enabled him to consecrate two bishops, his claims were still looked on with suspicion, and it is said that when the legates were in England they pronounced the papal condemnation of his pretensions. Wulfstan would not be consecrated by him, and he was not allowed to hallow Harold's church at Waltham, or Eadward's new minister, or to place the crown on Harold's head. England was held to be involved in his schism. Robert was not the man to let his wrongs be forgotten, and they were reckoned among the causes that were alleged in justification of the Norman invasion.

The Papacy
and the
Conquest.

When, on Eadward's death, Harold was chosen king, the Norman duke, William, determined to enforce his claim to the throne. He was careful to enlist the sympathy of Christendom; he appealed to the religious feelings of the age by declaring that Harold had forsworn himself on the relics of saints, and he sent an ambassador to lay his claim before Pope Alexander II. and ask his approval. He thus constituted the Pope the arbiter of his claim to the English throne; and he did so at a time when the Roman see was under the guidance of the mastermind of the Archdeacon Hildebrand, afterwards Gregory VII. William's ambassador, no doubt, insisted strongly on his master's declaration that if he was successful he would reform the ecclesiastical condition of the country. We may gather from later events that the duke promised that Peter's pence should be paid regularly, and we are told that he even declared that he would consider the kingdom a grant from St. Peter. Harold sent no one to plead his cause; nevertheless many of the cardinals urged that the Holy See ought not to sanction bloodshed. Hildebrand, however, upheld the duke's request. With him the greatness of the papacy outweighed all other considerations. England was held to be an undutiful daughter of Rome. Her king, Harold, had visited Rome in Benedict's time, and had acknowledged the schismatical Pope, and her chief bishop had received the pall from him; political interests governed the affairs of the English Church; the papal authority was lightly regarded, and prelates whose appointments had been confirmed at Rome were deprived of their sees by the national assembly. Hildebrand's arguments prevailed; and in after-days the cardinals blamed him for thus making the Holy See a party to the destruction of so many lives. Alexander sent the duke a ring and a consecrated banner, and the conquest of England was undertaken as a Holy War. This gives special significance to the night spent in prayer by the invading host, to the presence of many clergy in William's army, and to the early mass at which he received the Holy Elements. In the battle the duke wore hanging from his neck the relics to which Harold is said to have done despite. The Dragon of Wessex sank before the papal banner, and the standard of Harold was sent to the Pope in exchange for his gift.

Summary:
the national
character of
the Church
before the
Norman
Conquest.

Although the close union of the Church with the State during the period before the Conquest had some ill effects on the character of the clergy, it gave the Church a firm hold on the people. The use that it made of its influence on society lies apart from the main purpose of this book; yet some notices have been given of its efforts for social reformation. From it came all that there was of purity, gentleness, and humanity in the life of the people. By example and precept it taught the rich their duty towards the poor, it educated all who cared to learn, it purified domestic life, it exalted the position of woman and protected her weakness, it shielded the helpless from oppression, and proclaimed that the slave was precious in the sight of God. The clergy recommended the manumission of slaves as a meritorious deed; the ceremony was often performed at the altar of a church, and records of such acts are recorded in the missal-books of minsters. When a king or noble visited some church, it was held that the visitor paid a high compliment to the clergy if he freed a slave or a captive before their altar. The national character of the Church deeply affected the life of the State. Its unity in a large measure gave unity to the people, and created the nation. Its ministers held each his recognized place in the national organization; the parish priest, as the head of the parish, attended the hundred-court with the reeve of the lord; the bishop was a member of the national council, and sat with the ealdorman in the local courts. Great as the political power of the bishops was, they made no attempt to strengthen their temporal position at the expense of the national system; they did not seek to become territorial princes, like the bishops of the Continent, who held a position derived from the arrangements of the Roman Empire. This is true even of the two archbishops, though the high degree of temporal power attached to their sees is signified by the right they exercised of coining money. For, while the archbishops of Canterbury succeeded to much of the power once held by the under-kings of the Kentish kingdom, they did not use it in attempts to build up a subordinate princedom; and if the archbishops of York appear for a season as independent political leaders of the Northern people, they cease to do so when their province is thoroughly united to the dominions of the English king. In the midst of the struggles of contending parties and the treason of ambitious nobles, the English prelates continued faithfully to fulfil their duties to the State, and the clergy at large supplied it with a succession of able administrative officials. Churchmen bore their share of the national burdens. The fleets with which the king and the witan sought to guard the coasts were raised by levies from every shire. To these levies the lands of the Church were liable equally with those of laymen. Accordingly we find that Archbishop Ælfric, at his death in 1005, was possessed of ships and their equipments, the quota, no doubt, that he was bound to furnish when the witan decided on gathering a fleet. His best ship together with armour for sixty men he left to the king, and, besides this, he gave a ship to the people of Kent, and another to the people of Wiltshire— probably to help them to bear the burden that the war laid upon them. Moreover, the Danegeld, which was originally raised for the purpose of buying peace of the Danes, and was continued as a permanent tax on every hide of cultivated land until it was abolished by the Confessor, to be reimposed in a more oppressive form by the Norman Conqueror, was paid, except in cases of special exemption, on the lands of ecclesiastics as well as of laymen.

The freedom of the Church kept alive the national spirit in the evil days that followed the Conquest; it was used to restrain oppression, and the Church became the bond that united conquerors and conquered in one people. As regards the Church itself, its national character gave it independence, and in many ways it acted by itself apart from the rest of Western Christendom. From the reign of the Mercian Cenwulf to the reign of the Confessor it was virtually free from papal interference, and the Popes took little heed of what passed in England. It made saints of those who were venerated by the English people, and observed their mass-days in accordance with the decrees of the national council; it constantly used the tongue of the people in prayers and homilies; its doctrines were held and advanced with little reference to papal authority, and its rights were laid down by kings and enforced by civil officers. Isolated from the rest of Europe, England seemed to men like another world, of which the archbishop of Canterbury was pope. The isolation and strongly national character of the Church were not without danger to its well-being. To be cut off from Rome was to lose all share in the manifold and progressive life of Western Christendom. Had the Church of England retained its purely insular character, it would never have risen much above the level of the nation, nor have been able to elevate society. During the years immediately preceding the Conquest it sank with the nation. It was a period of exhaustion both in Church and State; and the time might have come when the isolation of the Church of England would have ended in a decay as complete as that of the Celtic Church. From such a danger the Church was saved by the Norman Conquest. It rested with the Conqueror and his successors to determine how far the Conquest was to lead to the fulfilment of Hildebrand's expectations, to decide whether England should become the submissive handmaid of Rome.

CHAPTER V.

ROYAL SUPREMACY.

THE CONQUEROR AND LANFRANC—
CANTERBURY AND YORK—
SEPARATE ECCLESIASTICAL
SYSTEM—REMOVAL OF SEES—
EXTENT AND LIMITS OF
PAPAL INFLUENCE—THE
CONQUEROR'S
BISHOPS—CHANGE IN THE
CHARACTER OF THE CHURCH—AN
APPEAL TO ROME—FEUDAL
TENDENCIES—ST. ANSELM—
STRUGGLE AGAINST TYRANNY—
INVESTITURES—HENRY I.—
COUNCILS—LEGATES—
INDEPENDENCE OF THE SEE OF
YORK—SUMMARY.

Deposition
of English
prelates.

In order to ensure the success of his invasion, William had given the Pope a strong claim on his obedience, at a time when the papal power was advancing rapidly under the guidance of Hildebrand, who in 1073 became Pope with the title of Gregory VII. Nevertheless William succeeded in using the papal pretensions to strengthen his hold on England, and in disregarding them when they threatened to weaken his absolute sovereignty in Church and State. In 1070, when he had completed the conquest of the land, he set about securing the submission of the Church, and invited Alexander II. to send legates to his court. Accordingly certain legates visited this country, and deposed Stigand and other bishops and abbots. Thus the Pope was gratified by the deposition of the uncanonical archbishop, while the Conqueror, by ousting the native prelates, crushed the strongest element of national resistance. York, which was vacant by the death of Ealdred, was given to Thomas of Bayeux, one of the king's clerks; other Normans were appointed to different sees; Lanfranc, archbishop of Canterbury, 1070-1089. and shortly afterwards Lanfranc was appointed to Canterbury. Lanfranc, a native of Pavia, a man of great learning and ability, and especially skilled in civil law, first came to Normandy as a teacher. He suddenly gave up this work, entered the newly founded monastery of Bec, and devoted himself to the monastic life. He became prior, and his talents attracted the notice of the duke, who made him his counsellor, and gave him the abbacy of his new monastery, St. Stephen's, at Caen. At Rome, Lanfranc was honoured as the defender of transubstantiation, and his appointment to Canterbury was warmly approved by the Pope. He was a man on whom the Conqueror could safely rely for the furtherance of his ecclesiastical policy. Hitherto there had virtually been only one system of administration for both Church and State. William's work was to create a separate ecclesiastical system, carried on by clerical officers. Yet the Church no less than the State was to be under his own absolute control; and so, while he needed a strong archbishop, he needed one who would exert his strength to maintain and increase the royal power. In Lanfranc he found an archbishop after his own heart, in exalting whose position he strengthened his own.

Canterbury
and York.

No writ was issued for the consecration of Thomas of York until Lanfranc had received consecration, and this delay was perhaps intentional; for when Thomas brought the writ to Lanfranc he was bidden to profess obedience to the see of Canterbury. He refused to do so, on the ground that Gregory had instituted two co-ordinate archbishoprics. On the other hand, the bishops of York, from Paulinus to Ecgberht, had not enjoyed metropolitan dignity, and even since Ecgberht's time the see had occupied an inferior position to Canterbury. Lanfranc had papal decrees and other evidences on his side, and gained the king's support by representing that an independent metropolitan at York might crown an independent king of Northumbria. William compelled Thomas to profess obedience to Lanfranc personally, and, with respect to the future, ordered that the question should be decided by the Pope. When the two archbishops went to Rome for their palls, Alexander was about to degrade Thomas and Remigius, bishop of Dorchester, who went with them, on account of canonical irregularity, and only forbore to do so at Lanfranc's request. Thomas brought forward the matter of the profession, and further claimed Dorchester, Lichfield, and Worcester as subject to York. Alexander referred these matters to the decision of an English synod, and the case seems to have been heard before a mixed assembly of clergy and laity, which pronounced against Thomas; he was forced to make a general profession of obedience, the Humber was declared the boundary between the provinces, and he was left with only one suffragan, the bishop of Durham. This disproportion between the archbishoprics had not been contemplated by Gregory, for his division, which was based on the assumption that the whole island was under one rule, included Scotland in the province of York. Under William and Lanfranc the English Church made its power felt in yet unconquered Celtic lands. The claim of York was asserted over Scotland. As that country had no metropolitan and no organized episcopal system, the assertion was plausible, and a bishop of the Orkneys was certainly consecrated by Thomas. It is extremely doubtful whether the authority of Canterbury was in any instance acknowledged in Wales during this reign, though a few years later it was, as we shall see, successfully asserted. In Ireland the irregular condition of the episcopacy naturally led kings and bishops to look up to Lanfranc; he consecrated two archbishops of Dublin, who made profession to him, and he wrote with authority to two kings on matters of discipline. An approach was thus made to the ecclesiastical submission of Ireland, and the primate of Britain was not unreasonably held by Latin Christendom to be "Patriarch of the nations beyond the sea."

National
synods and
ecclesiastical
courts.

Under William and Lanfranc synods were again held frequently, and, in accordance with the king's policy, ecclesiastical legislation, which had in the preceding age been provided for in the national assembly, was confined to them. They were councils of the whole Church; for the archbishop of Canterbury was acknowledged as primate of all Britain: they consisted of one house, and such of the inferior clergy as attended them were little more than spectators, for no one might speak without special permission save bishops and abbots. Their action was controlled by the king, and we find them held at the same place as, and immediately after the close of, one or other of the yearly meetings of the great council. Episcopal elections seem to have been made in these synods instead of in the national assembly, though in these, as in all else, the king was supreme. While the Church thus regained separate synodical activity, the bishops did not lose their places in the national assembly. Their right, however, no longer rested simply on the wisdom supposed to be inherent in their office; they now held their temporalities as baronies, and sat in the council as barons; for the old witenagemót had been transformed into a feudal council. A separation was also effected in the judicial system. The Conqueror declared the union of civil and ecclesiastical jurisdiction to be mischievous, and provided that henceforth no bishop or archdeacon should sit in the hundred court; that all spiritual causes should be tried by the bishop in his own court and be determined according to the canons, and that if any one disobeyed the bishop's summons and remained contumacious after excommunication, he should be brought to obedience by the king or the sheriff. This establishment of ecclesiastical courts, with their own system of law, was doubtless pleasing to the Pope, for the old English practice was contrary to the spirit of Hildebrand's work. Its ultimate tendency was to lead men to look to Rome as the supreme court of appeal in spiritual causes, and to set churchmen in opposition to the Crown. For some time after the Conqueror's death the separation of the courts was not fully effected, and this tendency was scarcely apparent. Nevertheless, his policy raised up a power in England that in later days greatly hampered the exercise of the royal authority and brought some troubles on the country.

Removal of
  sees.

Among the more important synodical decrees of this reign is that of the council held at London in 1075, which ordered that bishops' sees should be removed from villages to cities. The change begun by Leofric was carried fully out now that nearly every bishop was a foreigner. The see of Sherborne was moved by Hermann to Salisbury (Old Sarum), to be moved again when the present church of the new Salisbury was built in the reign of Henry III.; the see of Selsey was moved to Chichester; that of Lichfield to Chester, and a few years later to Coventry, where the bishop seized on the abbey by force; the see of Elmham was moved first to Thetford, and then to Norwich; and in the reign of Rufus, the bishop of Wells left his little city for Bath. While the decrees of ancient Popes and councils were cited as authorities for this measure, the act of the council, like all the conciliar acts of the reign, derived its force from the king's approval.

Extent of
  papal
influence.

Gregory had reason to congratulate himself on the part he had taken in forwarding the Conquest. The uncanonical archbishop was deposed, and his place taken by one who was especially pleasing to the Holy See; insular peculiarities were removed, the new foreign bishops were far more amenable to papal influence than the native bishops had been, and the changes effected in the government of the Church were generally such as he approved. In these and some other matters his desires were in accord with the policy of the Conqueror. Where it was otherwise he found that the king and his archbishop would act according to their own judgment. While Lanfranc cordially sympathized in Gregory's attempt to root out the custom of clerical marriage, his action was governed by the circumstances of the Church over which he presided. In England the custom obtained too widely to be attacked without discrimination. Accordingly the Council of Winchester, in 1076, only partially followed the example of the council which Gregory had held in Rome two years before. It decreed that no canon should have a wife, that the marriage of priests was for the future forbidden, and that no bishop should ordain a married man deacon or priest. On the other hand, priests who were already

57

married were not called upon to leave their wives. Other decrees of this council insisted on the sanctity of marriage, and the necessity of obtaining the Church's blessing in matrimony.

Its limits.

The absolute supremacy of the Conqueror in ecclesiastical matters is expressed in three rules which he is said to have laid down, and which define his rights in relation to the papacy. He would have no Pope acknowledged as apostolic without his bidding, and no papal letters brought into his kingdom unless he approved them. Synodical decrees were to have no force unless he had first ordained them; and none of his barons or officers of state were to be excommunicated or subjected to ecclesiastical rigour without his precept. Nor did he hesitate to return a flat refusal to a papal demand; for when Gregory sent a legate to admonish him to be more punctual in forwarding Peter's pence, and to demand a profession of fealty to the Holy See, he wrote that he admitted the one claim and not the other. Fealty he would not do, for he had not promised it, nor did he find that earlier kings had done it. He took his stand on his position as king of England; that which his predecessors had done he would do, but he would not grant the Pope any authority over his kingdom that they had not granted. Even Gregory was forced to suffer this; he seems to have blamed Lanfranc for the king's independent answer, bade him come to Rome, and urged him to bring William to obedience. Lanfranc defended himself in becoming terms, but stayed where he was, and at last the Pope threatened to suspend him if he did not obey his summons. Gregory, however, had powerful enemies nearer home, and did not care to quarrel with a king who steadily refused to take part against him. His struggle with Henry IV. gave occasion for the exercise, perhaps for the enunciation, of the first of the Conqueror's rules, and Lanfranc writes that "our island" had not yet decided between Gregory and the antipope Clement. Lanfranc's own sympathies, of course, were with Gregory, but he would not condemn the action of the Emperor; he thought that the proper attitude for England was one of neutrality.

Norman
bishops.

With the exception of Worcester, no English see was left in the hands of a native bishop. They were held either by Normans or by the Lotharingians who had been appointed in the Confessor's reign. At Worcester, Wulfstan, though not a man of learning, was allowed to retain his bishopric on account of his holiness. Among his other good works, he preached in Bristol against the slave-trade with Ireland that was largely carried on there, and persuaded the townsmen to give it up. Most of William's bishops were men of high character, for his appointments were free from simony, and were, no doubt,

58

suggested by Lanfranc; and the king himself had no liking for evil men. Some of them were learned; nearly all were magnificent. They did not play a great part in State affairs, and stand in some contrast both to the old native bishops, who were leaders of the witan, and, though several of them had been the king's clerks, to the bishops of a later period, who were before all things royal ministers. They generally rebuilt their churches in the Norman style, of which the Confessor's church at Westminster was the earliest example in England. At York, Archbishop Thomas did away with the discipline introduced by Ealdred, and assigned separate prebends to each of the canons, an arrangement which was gradually adopted in all cathedral churches with secular chapters. That the chapter of a cathedral church should consist of monks was extremely rare except in England, but as the Normans generally were strong supporters of monasticism, this was a peculiarity of which they approved, and in some churches secular canons were displaced by monks. Some of the bishops, however, who were not monks, with Walchelin, bishop of Winchester, at their head, saw that monastic chapters were a hindrance to the bishop, and were unfitted for their duties. They conceived the idea of replacing the monks by secular canons even in the metropolitan church. William is said to have approved of the scheme; but it was highly distasteful to Lanfranc, "the father of the monks," and he obtained a letter from Alexander II. indignantly forbidding it. The scheme was defeated, and Walchelin, who had forty clerks with their tonsure cut and their dress prepared as canons, ready to take the place of the monks of St. Swithun's, and to divide the monastic estates into prebends, had to send them about their business. Although William's Norman bishops were generally good specimens of continental churchmen, they had no sympathy with the thoughts and feelings of their clergy and people. Of one only, Osbern of Exeter, it is said that he adopted the English mode of life. Lanfranc despised the national saints, and doubted the right of his predecessor, Ælfheah, to the title of martyr, until he was taught better by Anselm, abbot of Bec. The admiration of the Normans for monasticism caused a considerable increase in the practice of endowing monasteries with tithes and parish churches, and thus in many cases tithes were paid to abbeys both here and abroad.

The national character of the Church.

In every respect our Church lost much of its insular, and something also of its national, character by the Conquest. Its prelates were foreigners; it was drawn more closely to Rome, and legates came over, and judged and deposed her native bishops, not always justly; its councils and courts were separated from the councils and courts of the nation. There seems to have been a change made even in doctrine; for the dogma of transubstantiation, of which Lanfranc was the special champion, was now universally accepted, and the archbishop's eagerness in this matter is reflected in the many stories of miracles connected with the Holy Elements which appear in contemporary literature. Yet the Church remained the representative of English nationality; her influence at once began to turn Normans into Englishmen; and it is interesting to find Lanfranc using the terms "our island" and "we English," and describing himself to Alexander II. as a "new Englishman." As primate of the English Church, he was the spiritual head of the nation, of English villeins as well as of Norman barons. All were Englishmen to him, and all soon became in truth one people. And while the establishment of a separate system of ecclesiastical administration tended to destroy the national character of the Church, this tendency was neutralized by the exercise of the king's supremacy. The new system worked well; but its success was due to the fact that it was carried out by a king and a primate at once so strong and so united in policy as the Conqueror and Lanfranc.

William
Rufus,
1087-1100.

The first William, if an austere man, was a mighty ruler, who loved order and valued the services of good men: the second was a braggart and a blasphemer, whose life was unspeakably evil and whose greediness knew no shame. In his hands the royal supremacy became a hateful tyranny, and the relations between the Church and the Crown were disturbed. Early in the reign the change in these relations was illustrated by an appeal to Rome. William of Saint-Calais, bishop of Durham, an ambitious and crafty intriguer, was cited to appear before the king's court on a charge of treason, and his lands were seized. He complained that his bishopric had been seized, and Lanfranc, who upheld the king's action, answered that his fiefs were not his bishopric. Next he pleaded the privilege of his order, and refused to be judged by the lay barons. "If I may not judge you and your order to-day," said Robert of Meulan, "you and your order shall never judge me." If bishops refused the jurisdiction of the king's court, they should cease to be members of it, they should no longer hold fiefs of the Crown. Finally, William appealed to Rome. Archbishop Robert had in exile appealed to the Pope against a decree of the national assembly; Bishop William, for the first time since the days of Wilfrith, made a like appeal in the presence of the king and his council. The sole object of Rufus was to obtain Durham Castle; the bishop surrendered it, and was allowed to go abroad, but he does not appear to have prosecuted his appeal.

Feudal
tyranny.

The special danger which threatened the Church in this reign arose from the attempt to treat it as a feudal society. Ralph Flambard, the minister of Rufus, raised money for his master chiefly by exaggerating and systematizing the feudal elements already existing in civil life. The practice of granting the temporalities by investiture shows that, even before the Conquest, Church lands were to some extent regarded in a feudal light, and since then this idea had gained strength. Rufus treated them as mere lay fiefs, and dealt with the prelates simply as his tenants-in-chief. No profits could, of course, accrue to the Crown from Church lands, such as were gathered from lay fiefs in the form of reliefs, a payment made by the heir on entering on his estate, or from other feudal burdens of a like kind. When, therefore, a bishopric or royal abbey fell vacant, the king, to compensate himself for the disparity, instead of causing the property to be administered for the benefit of the Church, entered on the lands and treated them as his own. It thus became his interest to keep sees vacant until he received a large sum for them. Simony grew prevalent and the character of the clergy declined; they engaged in secular pursuits, farmed the taxes, and sought in all ways to make money. After the death of Lanfranc in 1089, the king kept the archbishopric vacant, and granted the lands of the see to be held by his friends or by the highest bidder. This was a different matter from his dealings with other sees; for the archbishop was the spiritual head of the nation, and constitutionally the chief adviser of the king and the foremost member of his court, as he had been of the witenagemót. Accordingly the barons saw the king's conduct with displeasure. Rufus was not moved by greediness alone. While Lanfranc lived he had been forced to listen to his remonstrances with respect, and as he hated reproof, he determined not to appoint another archbishop as long as he could avoid doing so. He would, he declared to one of his earls, be archbishop himself. Neither the suffragan bishops nor the monks of Christ Church dreamed of electing without his order, and each year the state of the Church grew worse. At last Rufus fell sick and was like to die. Then the bishops and nobles entreated him, for his soul's sake, to appoint a primate and do other works meet for repentance. He consented willingly, and they sent for Abbot Anselm, who chanced to be in England.

S. Anselm,
archbishop,
1093-1109.

Anselm was a native of Aosta. Born and brought up amid the cloud-capt Alps, he longed when a child to climb the mountains and find God's house, which, he had been told, was in the clouds. One night he dreamed that he had done so and had found the palace of the Great King: he sat at the Lord's feet and told Him how grieved he was that His handmaids were idling in the harvest-fields below. Then, at the Lord's bidding, the steward of the palace gave him bread of the purest whiteness, and he ate and was refreshed. The dream is told us by his friend and biographer, Eadmer, who no doubt heard it from his own lips. It was prophetic of his life and character. He grew up studious and holy; his learning was renowned through Europe, and by Lanfranc's advice he entered the monastery of Bec, and became abbot there. He visited England more than once, and men marvelled to see how the stern Conqueror became gentle when he was by. When he was brought to the sick-bed of Rufus he received his confession and urged him to amend his life. The king, who thought that he was dying, promised to do so, and his lords begged him to begin by naming an archbishop. He raised himself in his bed, and pointing to Anselm, said, "I name yonder holy man." There seems to have been no form of election; the king's word was held a sufficient appointment. Anselm was sorely unwilling to accept the office; he believed that the king would recover, and he knew his evil heart. To make him archbishop was, he said, "to yoke an untamed bull and an old and feeble sheep together." He told Rufus that if he consented, the grants made during the vacancy of the lands of the see must be revoked, and that he must take him as "his spiritual father and counsellor;" for such was the constitutional position of the primate with respect to the king. Lastly, he reminded the king that he had already acknowledged Urban II. as Pope; for Rufus had not yet decided between the two claimants for the papacy.

The
untamed
bull and the
feeble
sheep.

Before Anselm's consecration the king recovered, and turned back to his evil ways. He tried to make Anselm promise that he would not reclaim the lands of the see which he had granted out as knights' fees. To this Anselm could not agree, for he would not lessen the property of his church. Nevertheless he was consecrated, and did homage to the king, as the custom was. Before long Rufus wanted money for an expedition against Normandy. The archbishop offered £500. Rufus was advised to demand a larger sum, and sent the money back. His demand was evidently based on the idea that Anselm owed him much for making him archbishop; and Anselm, though willing to contribute to the king's need, rejoiced that now no one could assert that he had made a simoniacal payment, and gave the money to the poor. When Rufus was about to sail, Anselm asked to be allowed to hold a synod, and the wrathful king answered him with jeers: "What will you talk about in your council?" Anselm fearlessly replied that he would speak of the foul vices that infected the land, and named the special vice of the king and his court. "What good will that do you?" asked the king. "If it does me no good," was the answer, "I hope it will do something for God and for you." He prayed him to fill the vacant abbacies.

"Tush!" said the king, "you do as you will with your manors, and may I not do what I will with my abbeys?" In his eyes the rights of a patron were merely the rights of a lord over his lands. He left England in wrath with the archbishop. Anselm had not yet received the pall, and when the king came back he asked leave to go and fetch it. "From which Pope?" demanded the king; and Anselm answered, "From Urban." Now, though Rufus had no objection to acknowledge Urban, he did not choose that any one should decide the matter save himself. He took his stand upon his father's rule, and the rule was a good one, for the acknowledgment of a Pope was a matter of national policy. His fault lay in refusing to make his choice out of a sheer love of tyranny. A meeting of the great council was held at Rockingham to decide whether Anselm could maintain "his obedience to the Holy See without violating his allegiance to his earthly king." The king most unfairly treated him as though the question had been decided against him and he was contumacious. The bishops took part against him, and their conduct shows how deeply the feudal idea had sunk: they were the "king's bishops," and their counsel was due to him and not to their metropolitan. William of Saint-Calais, now in favour again, even advised the king to take away the archbishop's staff and ring, and at the king's bidding the bishops renounced their obedience to him. The nobles, however, would not become instruments of a tyranny that might strike next at themselves. "He is our archbishop," they said, "and the rule of Christianity in this land is his; and therefore we as Christians cannot, as long as we live, renounce his authority." The matter was adjourned; yet it was something that the tyrant had been shown that men recognized higher laws of action than the feudal principles by which he sought to make Church and State alike subservient to his caprices.

As evil ever strives to master good, so the Red King was set on mastering Anselm. To this end he acknowledged Urban, persuaded him in return to send the pall to him, and then offered the legate who brought it a large sum for the Pope if he would depose Anselm. When the legate refused his offer, he tried to make Anselm give him money for the pall. In this, of course, he failed, and the pall was placed by the legate on the high altar of Canterbury Minster, whence Anselm took it. The next year the king found a new cause of quarrel; the military tenants of the archbishopric serving in the Welsh war were badly equipped, and he bade Anselm be ready to answer for it in his court. Anselm then petitioned to be allowed to go to Rome, and urged his request in spite of the king's repeated refusals. His case was discussed at a meeting of the great council at Winchester. In persisting in his demand against the will of the king he was certainly acting contrary to the customs of the kingdom, and he was, if not in words, at least in fact, appealing to the Pope against the king. At the same time, it must be remembered that he had none to help him, and that he naturally turned to Rome as the place of strength and refreshment in his troubles. The bishops plainly told him: "We know that you are a holy man, and that your conversation is in Heaven; but we confess that we are hampered by our relations whom we support, and by our love of the manifold affairs of the world, and cannot rise to the height of your life." Would he descend to their level? "Ye have said well," he answered; "go, then, to your lord. I will hold me to God." Nor were the nobles on his side. At Rockingham his demand was in accordance with the customs of the realm; here the case was different. Rufus declared that he might go, but that if he went he would seize the archbishopric. He went, and the king did as he had said. Urban received the archbishop magnificently, styling him the "pope and patriarch of another world," and promising to help him. Council of Bari, 1098. At the Council of Bari the Pope called on him to defend the Catholic faith against the Greek heresy. His speech delighted the council; the conduct of Rufus was discussed, and it was decided that he ought to be excommunicated. Anselm, however, interceded for him, and his intercession availed. Although Urban in public spoke severely enough to a bishop whom Rufus sent to plead his cause, he talked more mildly in private; money was freely spent among the papal counsellors, and a day of grace was given to the king. It is scarcely too much to say that Anselm's cause was sold. He was present at the Lateran Council in 1099, where he heard sentence of excommunication decreed against all who conferred or received investiture; his wrongs were spoken of with indignation, but nothing was done to redress them. He left Rome convinced that he could never return to England while Rufus lived, and was dwelling at Lyons when he heard of the king's death.

Investitures.

In the first clause of the charter in which Henry I. declared the abolition of the abuses introduced by Rufus we read that he made "God's holy Church free;" he would "not sell it nor put it to farm," and he would take nothing from the demesne of bishopric or abbacy during a vacancy. He invited Anselm to return, and welcomed him joyfully. When, however, he called on him to do him homage on the restoration of his lands which Rufus had seized, Anselm refused; for he had laid to heart what he had heard at the Lateran council. It is evident that personally he had no objection to perform these acts, which he had already done to Rufus. His objection arose from the fact that they were now forbidden. Rome had spoken, and he felt bound to obey. As the question of Investitures forms the subject of a separate volume of this series, it will be enough to say here that the conveyance of the temporalities of a see was regarded in the feudal state as the chief thing in the appointment of a bishop, who received investiture of his office by taking the ring and crozier from the hands of the king—a ceremony which encouraged the feudalization of the

Church and gave occasion for many abuses. At the same time, it was by no means desirable that a prelate should hold wide lands and jurisdictions without entering into the pledge of personal loyalty required of other lords. With the abstract side of the question, however, Anselm was not concerned. With him it was a matter of obedience, and he held that he was bound to obey the Pope rather than the law of the land. For the king's demand was justified by the custom of England, and it was on this that he took his stand. "What," he said, "has the Pope to do with my rights? Those that my predecessors possessed in this realm are mine." Anselm would neither do homage nor consecrate the bishops elect who had received investiture. Yet the dispute was conducted with moderation on both sides. The archbishop in person brought his men to defend the king against the invasion of Robert; he forwarded Henry's marriage and crowned his queen; while Henry, even during the progress of the dispute, authorized him to hold a synod and sanctioned its decrees. Stern as the king was, he loved order and justice, and his conduct presents a striking contrast to the conduct of his brother.

The closer relations with Rome introduced by the Conquest compelled the king to attempt to gain the Pope's agreement to the English law. Paschal II., while bound to abide by the decision of the Lateran council, was evidently unwilling to alienate the king, and seems to have temporized. At last Anselm went to Rome, at the request of the king and the nobles, who no doubt hoped that he would learn there that the Pope was scarcely whole-hearted in the matter. His presence, however, seems to have stirred Paschal to give the king's envoy a flat refusal. Henry then took the archbishopric into his hands, and Anselm remained abroad. During his absence the king embarked on a piece of ecclesiastical administration. His constant want of money led him to levy a fine on all the clergy who had disobeyed the decree of Anselm's council by neglecting to put away their wives; and, finding the sum less than he calculated, he demanded a payment from every parish church. About two hundred priests, in their robes, waited on him barefoot, and prayed him to release them from this demand without success. At last, in 1107, the question of investitures was arranged between the king and the Pope, and the arrangement was sanctioned by a great council at London. The king gave up the investiture, and in return his right to homage was acknowledged. He may be said to have surrendered the shadow and to have secured the substance. While the chapters were allowed to choose the bishops, they were to exercise their right at the king's court, where, of course, they were subject to his influence. Anselm again received the temporalities, and the vacant bishoprics were filled up. Throughout the dispute the clergy remained loyal to the king in his struggle with the feudal lords, and the affairs of the Church went on as usual. The speedy and satisfactory settlement of a question that agitated the

Empire for half a century, and the moderate spirit in which it was debated, were mainly due to the character of the king; for Henry was a statesman of fertile genius, and, unlike Rufus, acted on well-defined principles. He was willing to grant the exact amount of freedom of action that seemed necessary to orderly development, while, at the same time, he kept that freedom in strict subordination to his own supremacy.

Acting on these principles, he allowed councils to be held, though, like his father, he made ecclesiastical legislation dependent on his sanction. At Anselm's synod, held at Westminster in 1102, a return was made to the old English custom of the joint action of the clergy and laity; for the nobles took part in it along with the bishops and abbots. Synodical activity under Henry I. The suspension of synodical action during the reign of Rufus had weakened the authority of the Church, and it was thought advisable that both orders should act together in legislation. The first canon marks the growth of ecclesiastical jurisdiction consequent on the separation of the courts. Archdeacons had now become judicial officers over distinct territorial divisions, and as the profits of their courts were considerable, it became necessary to decree that they should not be farmed. An advance was made on Lanfranc's legislation on clerical marriage; married priests and deacons were now ordered to put away their wives, an order which, as we have seen, was widely disregarded; no married man was to be admitted to the subdiaconate; tithes were not to be paid except to churches, and several decrees were made for the maintenance, dress, and general conduct of the clergy. Another national council, held in 1127, sat in the church of Westminster while the king held his court in the palace; just as now the Convocation of the Province of Canterbury and the High Court of Parliament are summoned to meet at the same time at Westminster.

Henry, like his father, aimed at establishing perfect harmony between Church and State, keeping both alike in absolute dependence upon himself. Accordingly he resisted any unauthorized interference on the part of the Pope with the affairs of the Church. Early in the reign a Burgundian archbishop landed here without invitation, claiming legatine authority over the whole kingdom. His claim was pronounced "unheard of." Although the Conqueror had invited the Pope to send him legates for a specified purpose, the archbishop of Canterbury was held to be the permanent representative of the Holy See in England, a *legatus natus*, whose authority was not to be superseded by a special legate, or *legatus a latere*. No one acknowledged the legate's authority, and "he went back," Eadmer remarks, "as he came." A more serious attempt to override the rights of the Church was made in the time of Anselm's successor, Ralph. The king was in Normandy, and when it became known that a legate, Anselm's nephew and namesake, was on his way hither, the bishops and nobles of the kingdom met in council, and sent Ralph over to Henry to request that he "would bring the innovation to nought," and the king prevented the legate Anselm from landing. In the time of the next archbishop, William of Corbeuil, Henry was, for political reasons, anxious to stand well with Rome, and accordingly admitted into the kingdom a legate from Honorius II., named John of Crema. Men saw with indignation that this legate sat in the highest seat in the metropolitan church, and said mass in the archbishop's stead, clad in episcopal vestments, though he was only a priest; "for both England and other countries knew that, from St. Augustin onwards, the archbishops were held to be primates and patriarchs, and were never made subject to a Roman legate." At the same time, though John occupied the seat of honour at the council of 1125, the summons ran in the name of the archbishop and the decrees were confirmed by the king. While, then, the Crown, the English Church, and the papal representative acted concurrently, the royal authority was saved. It was not so with the see of Canterbury or with the national interests it represented, and the archbishop went to Rome to complain of the injury done to his see. Honorius silenced his complaints by giving him a legatine commission, a measure which, while gratifying William personally, lessened the inherent dignity of his see and the independence of the Church.

Thurstan, archbishop of York, 1119-1140.

In spite of various efforts, the archbishops of York had hitherto been unable to evade the profession of obedience to Canterbury. Thurstan, the fourth since the Conquest, was a man of different mould from his predecessors, and refused to make the profession. Archbishop Ralph accordingly refused to consecrate him, and the king upheld the right of the primatial see, bidding Thurstan do what was due according to ancient usage. Thurstan was encouraged in his revolt by Popes Paschal II. and Calixtus II., who treated it as a good opportunity for a covert attack on the greatness of the English primate. The see of York remained vacant for about five years. At last Thurstan obtained leave from the king to attend the council held by Calixtus at Rheims, promising that he would not accept consecration from the Pope, while Calixtus undertook that he would do nothing to the prejudice of the see of Canterbury. Nevertheless Thurstan received consecration from Calixtus, and so escaped making the profession. Henry refused to allow him to return to England; and the next Pope, Honorius II., seems to have actually declared the kingdom under an interdict, though the sentence was not published here. The dispute went on for some years, and the old question appears even now to excite the local patriotism of some of the clergy of York. Yet it can scarcely be denied that Thurstan sacrificed the interests of the national Church to the aggrandizement of his see, and that both he and Calixtus got the better of the king by a somewhat discreditable trick. York was freed for ever from the obligation of obedience by a bull of Calixtus.

Scottish and
 Welsh
bishoprics.

One phase of the quarrel between Canterbury and York concerned the Scottish bishops. On a vacancy of the see of St. Andrews, Alexander, king of Scots, was induced to write to Ralph of Canterbury, asking him to recommend a new bishop, and reminding him that the bishops of St. Andrews were always consecrated by the Pope or the archbishop of Canterbury, which was, of course, the reverse of the truth, for they were suffragans of York. Ralph highly approved of this new doctrine, and in course of time Eadmer, the historian, a monk of Canterbury, was duly elected. Meanwhile, however, Alexander had changed his mind, and commanded Eadmer to receive consecration from Thurstan. This he refused to do, for he was heart and soul a Canterbury man, and after much disputing, he was forced to return to his convent unconsecrated. The dispute between Canterbury and York encouraged some of the Scottish bishops to revolt against Thurstan, whose authority was upheld by Calixtus. This quarrel is memorable because the Pope accepted Thurstan's theory that the king of Scots was the man of the king of England for Scotland, and not, as the Scots held, merely for Lothian or any other fief: in other words, he declared Scotland a vassal kingdom, a decision that became of importance later on. The question of canonical subjection was debated between St. Andrews and York, until, in 1188, Clement III. declared the Scottish Church immediately dependent on the Holy

68

See. The upshot of these disputes was, that the archbishops of Canterbury ceased to be the "primates and patriarchs of Britain," for York was freed from dependence upon them, and their attempt to extend their jurisdiction over Scotland utterly failed. On the other hand, the authority of Canterbury was established in Wales by the election to the see of St. David's of the Norman Bernard, who received consecration from Archbishop Ralph, and made profession to him.

Summary.

The ecclesiastical system of the Norman kings may be summed up as a generally successful attempt to give the Church power of action apart from the State, so far as was consistent with the supremacy of the Crown. Under Rufus this system became a mere means of tyranny; and among the many glories that attend the memory of St. Anselm, not the least is that he delivered the Church from the domination of the feudal idea, which would have destroyed her spirituality and left her helpless before the royal power. By the Conqueror and Henry I. the supremacy was used to establish harmony of action between Church and State, and to preserve the national character of the Church. Nevertheless the new relations with Rome introduced by the Conquest began to bear fruit in Henry's time, for on all occasions, both by the grant of legatine commissions and by upholding the pretensions of York, the Popes strove to depress the primatial see and to increase their own authority in England.

Although Henry had none of the brutal contempt for law that distinguished his brother, he was not less despotic, and his policy towards the Church differed from that pursued by his father in that, while the Conqueror made her co-ordinate under himself with the State, he degraded her to the position of a servant. He kept the see of Canterbury vacant for five years after the death of Anselm; all ecclesiastical matters were governed by political or personal considerations rather than with an eye to the true interests of the Church, and Henry was not above making money from ecclesiastical appointments. His chief adviser was Roger, bishop of Salisbury, an able minister and a magnificent noble, who owed his preferment to his administrative talents; for Henry employed clerical ministers, partly because he was thus enabled to secure men who had received a regular official training as royal clerks, and partly, no doubt, because their celibacy made it less likely that they would put their authority to a dangerous use. He rewarded them with bishoprics and other preferments, and thus secularized the Church in order to make her serve the State. At the same time, his reign saw the beginning of a movement that was destined to revive her spiritual character, and by that revival to increase her power and dignity. This quickened influence was due to the higher life that followed the introduction of the Cistercian rule.

CHAPTER VI.

CLERICAL PRETENSIONS.

STEPHEN AND THE ENGLISH CHURCH
—ARCHBISHOP THEOBALD AND
HENRY OF WINCHESTER—THOMAS
THE CHANCELLOR—THE SCUTAGE
OF TOULOUSE—THOMAS THE
ARCHBISHOP—CLERICAL
IMMUNITY—THE ARCHBISHOP IN
EXILE—HIS MARTYRDOM—
HENRY'S GENERAL RELATIONS TO
THE CHURCH—CONQUEST OF
IRELAND—RICHARD'S CRUSADE—
LONGCHAMP—ARCHBISHOP
HUBERT WALTER—CHARACTER OF
THE CLERGY.

Stephen's
accession,
1135.

Under the Norman dynasty the natural results of the Conqueror's ecclesiastical policy were controlled by the power of the Crown. Appeals to Rome were almost unknown; the principles which the Conqueror had laid down as defining the relations between the Crown and the papacy were maintained, and the establishment of ecclesiastical courts had not as yet proved mischievous; for in all serious cases the criminous clerk, after having been degraded by the spiritual judge, was handed over to the secular authority. Under a weak king, and then during a period of anarchy, the Church became invested with extraordinary power; her relations with Rome were increased, and new privileges were asserted which became dangerous to civil order. The weakness in Stephen's title was a moral one, for he and the nobles of the kingdom were pledged by oath to Matilda. His right then depended on a question that especially concerned the Church; and though he had received civil election, Archbishop William hesitated to crown him. His scruples were overcome, and the approval of the Church was secured by Henry, bishop of Winchester, Stephen's brother. Stephen was crowned, after swearing to maintain the liberty of the Church, and put forth a charter promising good government in general terms. The next year, at Oxford, the bishops swore fealty to him "as long as he should maintain the liberty and discipline of the

Church," a ceremony that may be described as a separate election by the Church, dependent on the king's conduct towards her. Stephen, who had received a letter of congratulation from Innocent II., now put forth a charter in which he recited his claims. As king by the grace of God, elected by the clergy and people, hallowed by William, archbishop and legate, and "confirmed by Innocent, pontiff of the Holy Roman See," he promised that he would avoid simony, and that the persons and property of clerks should be under the jurisdiction of their bishops. Thus, in order to strengthen his position, he not only gave prominence to the assent of the Church, but even cited the approval of the Pope, as though it conferred some special validity on the national election. This was, under the circumstances, the natural result of Duke William's petition that Rome would sanction his invasion, and justified Hildebrand's policy in espousing his cause.

The Battle
   of the
Standard,
   1138.

For a while the Church remained faithful to Stephen. The statesmen-bishops, Roger, the justiciar, and his nephews, the bishop of Ely, the treasurer, and the bishop of Lincoln, together with Bishop Roger's son, also called Roger, the chancellor, continued to carry on the administration. In the north a Scottish invasion was checked by the energy of the aged Archbishop Thurstan, who from his sick-bed stirred the Yorkshire men to meet the invaders. He was represented in the camp by his suffragan, the bishop of the Orkneys. The standard of the English army bore aloft the Host, and the figures of the patron saints of the three great Yorkshire churches, and the "Battle of the Standard," in which the Yorkshire men were completely victorious, had something of the character of a Holy War, in which the archbishop acted, as of old, as the natural head of the northern people.

The mischievous results of the appointment of Archbishop William as legate were apparent at his death; for Innocent granted a legatine commission, not to his successor, Theobald, but to Henry of Winchester. The authority of the see of Canterbury was thus grievously diminished, and the archbishop was made second to a resident representative of the Pope, one of his own suffragans. Stephen's quarrel with the Church. The abasement of Canterbury naturally drew the Church into greater dependence on Rome, and appeals, which had hitherto been almost unknown, became of constant occurrence. Equally unlike the justiciar, Roger of Salisbury, who devoted himself to secular administration and ambitions, and the churchmen who, full of the new fervour of the Cistercian movement, sought to raise the spiritual dignity of the Church, Henry of Winchester used his vast powers to exalt her temporal greatness. His jealousy for the privileges of the clergy brought him into collision with the king, who now by an act of extreme folly provoked a quarrel with the clerical order. Stephen suspected the loyalty of the bishop of Salisbury and his house, and caused him and the bishop of Lincoln to be arrested at Oxford. They were powerful lords and had reared several mighty castles. These they were forced to surrender by threats and ill-treatment. Stephen acted with the violence of a weak man; he had already lost the obedience of the barons, and the people must have learnt that his promises were not to be relied on; now he ensured his fall by offending the clergy. The legate summoned him to appear before a synod at Winchester, and the king of England actually appeared by his counsellor, Alberic de Vere, who made his defence. When he refused to restore the bishops' castles there was some talk of laying the case before the Pope. This he forbade, and yet appealed to Rome himself. At last he appeared before the legate stripped of his royal robes, and humbly received his censure "for having stretched out his hand against the Lord's anointed ones." Nevertheless the Church was alienated from him, and after his defeat at Lincoln the legate held another council at Winchester, and announced as its result that the majority of the clergy, "to whom the right of electing a prince chiefly belonged," had decided to transfer their allegiance to the Empress. The legate found that Matilda had little respect for the rights of the Church, and after a while turned against her. The result of these rapid changes was to destroy the unity of the clerical party.

The dispute
  about the
archbishopric
  of York.

Hitherto Archbishop Theobald had generally followed the legate's lead, and had played a secondary part in the affairs of the Church. In 1141, however, a cause of difference arose between them. The York chapter elected Stephen's nephew, William, to succeed Archbishop Thurstan. A minority of the chapter declared that simony and undue influence had been practised, and Theobald took their part, while Henry consecrated his nephew in spite of him. Anxious to put his power beyond the reach of fortune, the bishop of Winchester petitioned the Pope to make his see a third archbishopric. His request was refused, and his legatine commission expired in 1143, with the death of Innocent, the Pope who had granted it. Chief among the opponents of the new archbishop of York were the Cistercian abbeys of the north; and Bernard, abbot of Clairvaux, the head of the order, who was the guiding spirit of the papacy at this time, threw all his weight on their side. He disapproved of the diminution of the rights of Canterbury, and held that, in securing the see of York for their nephew, Stephen and Henry were injuring the Church to serve their own ends. Eugenius III. accordingly gave the legatine commission to

Theobald. Enraged at the opposition offered to Archbishop William by Henry Murdac, abbot of Fountains, his partizans sacked and burnt the abbey. As an answer to this outrage, Eugenius deprived William, and Murdac was elected archbishop by his authority, and received consecration from him. Stephen and Henry made a fatal mistake in matching themselves against the papacy, with Bernard and the whole Cistercian order at its back. They did not yield without a further struggle. Stephen forbade Theobald to attend the Pope's Council at Rheims in 1148. In spite of this prohibition he went to Rheims. Stephen banished him and seized his temporalities, until an interdict was laid upon the royal lands, and he was forced to be reconciled to him. Murdac made his position good at York. His rival, William, outlived him, was re-elected, and died a month after he had received the pall. During his retirement he led a holy and humble life, and after his death became the special saint of his church. Stephen had one more quarrel with Archbishop Theobald. He desired to have his son Eustace, an evil and violent man, crowned as his successor. This was forbidden by the Pope, and the primate and his suffragans refused the king's request. He tried to frighten them by shutting them in the house where they were consulting. The archbishop escaped across the Thames in a boat, and went abroad, and the king again seized the temporalities of the see.

Theobald,
Archbishop,
1139-1161.

Unlike Henry of Winchester, Theobald was guided by the new ideas which were born of the Cistercian revival. While desire for the secular greatness of the Church, her splendour and her wealth, led Henry to scheme and change sides according as he found Stephen or the Empress acting against her interests, Theobald sought a higher power for her, and attached himself to Bernard, who ruled Christendom by his sanctity and his intellectual gifts. Theobald's household was the home of a little society of men of like mind with himself. One of them was a young clerk of London, named Thomas, who soon became his chief adviser; another was John of Salisbury, who held a new office, that of the archbishop's secretary, or, as he would be called now, his chancellor; for Theobald saw that the archdeacons were by no means trustworthy officers, and appointed a secretary to control the administration of ecclesiastical law. This was a matter in which he took a deep interest, and the frequent appeals that were now made to Rome gave it a special importance. Study of civil law.In 1149 he brought over from Italy a doctor named Vacarius, and set him to give lectures at Oxford on the civil law, which supplied the method of procedure in ecclesiastical cases. In the next reign the study of the canon law, which was first systematized by Gratian of Bologna, was introduced into England, and then the clergy had a code as well as a method of procedure of their own. Stephen sent Vacarius out of the country, probably because he hated new things; but the study of the civil law could not be stopped so easily.

With aims and interests such as these, Theobald had no desire to see the anarchy which is generally called Stephen's reign prolonged. How terrible in some parts that anarchy was, when men "said openly that Christ and His saints slept," need not be described here. Some of the bishops rode to war and behaved like lay barons; others were held back by fear from censuring the ungodly. Nevertheless the Church still exhibited a pattern of order, and strove to restore peace to the kingdom. Although Theobald entered into no schemes for dethroning Stephen, he was fully convinced of the importance of securing the succession for Henry of Anjou. His counsellor, Thomas, now archdeacon of Canterbury, was urgent on the same side, and they were at last joined in their efforts after peace by Henry of Winchester. The chief obstacle was removed by the death of Eustace, and the Treaty of Wallingford soon followed. Henry II. owed his throne in no small degree to the support of the clergy.

Thomas the
Chancellor.

The young king chose for his chancellor Thomas, the archdeacon, to whose good offices he was much indebted. Thomas's father, Gilbert Becket, a wealthy trader, had been port-reeve of London. Thomas was sent to school at Merton priory, and was taken away from the school there while still young because his parents suffered serious losses. Nevertheless he was able to study at Paris, and after his return to England was often the companion of a rich noble named Richer de l'Aigle, who took him out hunting and hawking. As his father was now badly off, he became clerk to a merchant, whose name in English was Eightpenny, and after a while was introduced to the archbishop, entered his household, and soon became his most trusted adviser. He took orders, and received many rich preferments. As chancellor, he held one of the most important offices in the kingdom, and his duties brought him into constant companionship with the king, who treated him as an intimate friend. He was diligent in his secular work; he loved magnificence, and lived with grace and splendour. No chancellor had been so great a man before. He probably had a large share in the reorganization of the administrative machinery. One change was certainly due to him—the commutation of military service for a money payment. Taxation of ecclesiastical knights' fees. A step in this direction was made in 1156, when Henry laid a tax called scutage on Church lands held by knight's service. Theobald objected to this imposition, but his objections were fruitless. Three years later, when the king was undertaking a war in Toulouse, the chancellor advised him to take money from all who owed him military service, instead of calling upon them to go to

74

the war. The general importance of this measure does not belong to our subject; the scutage of Toulouse concerns us here simply because it was levied on church-lands. It excited far more indignation among the clergy than the earlier tax, because they saw that it was the beginning of a system, not an isolated expedient. The chancellor was held to have done the Church a grievous injury, and even his friends traced his later troubles to his sin against her.

When, in 1162, Henry bade his chancellor accept the primacy, he hoped to find him a powerful ally in carrying out the reforms he contemplated. Thomas assented unwillingly, for he was resolved, if he took the office, to maintain the claims of the Church to the utmost, and he knew that this would bring him into collision with the king. Although his life had been pure, it had not been clerical, and he had not even taken priest's orders when he was elected archbishop. He now entered on a new life. Everything that was then held becoming in a churchman and an archbishop he practised to the utmost. With the whole-heartedness with which he had thrown himself into his work as chancellor, he now, in a post that must have been less congenial to his nature, set himself to live up to the highest ideal then current of what an archbishop ought to be as regards both life and policy. He had enemies, for some were jealous of him, and some were honestly scandalized at his appointment. Ever regardless of the fear or favour of men, he added to their number by prosecuting the rights of his see to lands that had been alienated from it. In acting thus, his conduct, though perhaps injudicious, certainly became his office. His position as the head of the nation first brought him into opposition to the Crown. Henry wished that a certain tax, probably a survival of the Danegeld, which was paid to the sheriffs, should be brought into the royal revenue. The archbishop objected, no doubt because he thought that this would revive the old tax. "Saving your pleasure, lord king, we will not give it as revenue; but if the sheriffs and officers of the counties do their duty by us, we will never refuse it them by way of aid." The king was wroth. "By the eyes of God!" he cried, "it shall be given as revenue, and entered in the king's books; and you ought not to oppose me, for I am not oppressing any man of yours against your will." The archbishop answered, "By the eyes you have sworn by, my lord king, it shall not be levied from any of my lands, and from the lands of the Church not a penny!" He seems to have carried his point, and thus the first successful opposition to the will of the Crown in a financial matter proceeded from the Church of England. Nor was the archbishop slack in asserting the spiritual rights of his office; for he excommunicated one of the king's tenants-in-chief, and when Henry bade him absolve him, answered that it was not the king's business to say who should be bound and who unbound. In this matter the king demanded no more than the observance of one of the Conqueror's rules; the archbishop asserted no more than one of the eternal rights of the Church, which she had now become strong enough to claim.

Ecclesiastical
  discipline.

A greater conflict between the claims of the Crown and of the Church was at hand. The Conqueror had strengthened himself by increasing the power of the clergy; Henry could only establish the strong and orderly government he aimed at by lessening it. We have seen how rapidly clerical influence had grown during the anarchy owing to the suspension of the royal authority, the multiplication of appeals, the attention paid by Theobald to ecclesiastical law, and other causes. Clergy guilty of secular offences were tried solely by ecclesiastical courts; and as the spiritual judges, after inflicting an ecclesiastical penalty, refused to give up the clerical offender to a secular court, many gross crimes met with wholly inadequate punishments. For the number of persons in orders of different degrees was very large, and all alike claimed immunity from civil jurisdiction; and it is evident, though this was a matter of less consequence, that all offences against the clergy were also claimed as belonging to the province of the ecclesiastical courts.

Constitutions
  of
Clarendon,
  1164.

At a great council, held at Westminster in 1163, Henry asked if the bishops would obey the "customs of his grandfather," if they would agree that clerks convicted of secular crimes should, after degradation, be punished as laymen. The primate declared that clerks were not subject to the jurisdiction of an earthly king, and would only agree that a clerk already degraded should for another offence be punished by a lay judge. Henry asked the bishops if they would obey the "customs," and their reply, "Saving our order," was virtually a refusal. At a later interview he persuaded Archbishop Thomas to promise obedience to the customs unreservedly. He then summoned a council at Clarendon, and there, under strong pressure, the primate and his suffragans took the required pledge. The council then proceeded to inquire what the customs were, and a body of rules was drawn up called the "Constitutions of Clarendon." By these Constitutions all cases touching advowsons and presentations were to be tried in the king's court. The convicted clerk was no longer to be protected by the Church. Appeals from the archbishop were to be heard by the king, and were not to be carried further without his leave. Bishops and all who held of the Crown as by barony were to take part in the proceedings of the king's court until it came to sentence touching life or limb. Elections to bishoprics and royal abbeys were to be made by the higher clergy of the church in the king's chapel and with his assent, and the elect was to do homage and fealty to the king as his liege lord before he was consecrated. And the son of a villein was not to be ordained without his lord's leave. When the primate heard the Constitutions he refused to set his seal to them, declared he would not assent to them as long as he had breath in his body, and suspended himself from his sacred office until he had received the Pope's absolution from his hasty promise. The Constitutions, which were founded on the relations existing between the Church and the State in the reign of Henry I., were an attempt to bring matters back to a stage which had now been passed, to define relations that had hitherto been continually changing, and to establish a system which, however generally excellent, was contrary to the spirit of the age.

Council of
Northampton.

Archbishop Thomas twice tried to flee to the Pope, and failed through stress of weather or because the sailors were afraid of the king's anger. In October he was summoned to appear before the king's council at Northampton, and there an effort was made to crush him by multiplied suits. At last the king demanded an account of all the sums that had passed through his hands during his chancellorship, though he had already received a quittance. At Westminster and at Clarendon the bishops had sided, though timidly, with their primate, for the nature of the dispute forced them to do so. Now, when the whole business was reduced to a personal attack upon him, they sided with the king, just as their predecessors had done when Rufus attacked Anselm and Henry disputed with him. For though the pretensions of the Church limited the power of the Crown, and though Anselm and Becket each in his own day struggled for those pretensions, the bishops as a body were always on the king's side, for he had given them their office either because they had served him well, or because he expected them to be useful to himself. Accordingly Gilbert Foliot, bishop of London, a churchman of considerable worldly wisdom, who held that a quarrel with the king would injure the interests of the Church, advised the archbishop to submit to Henry, and other bishops said much the same. Thomas forbade them to sit in judgment on him, and appealed from his lay judges to the Pope. Before long he escaped from England, sorely against the king's will, and went to Pope Alexander III. at Sens, who at once condemned the Constitutions.

The

Alexander III. was in exile in France, for his rival, Victor, who was upheld by the Emperor Frederic I., was powerful in Italy, and he naturally held that it was more important to secure his own position than to uphold the English primate. He could not afford to offend Henry, lest he should take the side of the Emperor and his schismatical Pope. Accordingly he bade the archbishop keep silence for a while; and as Thomas did not think it seemly to stay in the dominions of Lewis of France, who was at enmity with Henry, he took up his abode in the Cistercian abbey of Pontigny, in Burgundy. When Victor died, in 1165, the Emperor set up another Pope, and made alliance with Henry, who was, perhaps, only saved from actively espousing the cause of the imperialist antipope by the wisdom of his justiciar, the earl of Leicester. Indeed, the ambassador he sent to the Emperor's council at Würzburg renounced the Pope in his master's name and promised that Henry would help Frederic's antipope. That year, however, Alexander returned to Rome, and felt himself strong enough to send the exiled primate a legatine commission. In virtue of this commission, Thomas in 1166 went to Vézelay, and there, in the abbey church, in the presence of a large congregation, excommunicated all the king's party, both clergy and laymen. He had heard that Henry was ill, and therefore did not excommunicate him. Nevertheless, with a voice choked with tears, he threatened him by name with a like sentence. In return, Henry so frightened the Cistercians that Thomas was virtually forced to leave Pontigny. This retaliation was as foolish as it was tyrannical; for the archbishop took shelter in France, and so gave Lewis a fresh means of annoying the English king. The details of the quarrel are intricate and somewhat wearisome. None of those concerned acted with dignity. Henry weakened his own position by appealing to the Pope to judge between him and one of his own subjects; he assented to the Pope's decrees when they were in his own favour, and resisted them when they were against him. Thomas was violent, and multiplied excommunications. Several efforts were made to bring about a reconciliation between him and Henry, and a meeting took place between them at Montmirail in 1169. The archbishop, however, would not be content with anything less than a complete surrender on the king's part, and the conference ended fruitlessly. Alexander sometimes upheld, and sometimes thwarted Thomas, just as his own interests dictated, and pursued a course that seemed to the stout-hearted archbishop mean and pusillanimous. "In the Roman court," he indignantly wrote, "Barabbas escapes and Christ is put to death." Lewis simply used the quarrel to his own advantage, and supported the archbishop just as he supported the lords of Henry's vassal states against him.

The
archbishop's

78

A new phase of the dispute arose from Henry's wish to have his eldest son crowned. The archbishop of Canterbury alone had the right to perform the ceremony; and when Thomas insisted on this right he was not contending for an empty honour; for coronation was held to be necessary to kingship, and it was the archbishop's duty to receive a pledge of good government from the king he crowned. Alexander first agreed to allow Roger of York to crown the young king, and, later, sent to prohibit him from doing so. Henry prevented the prohibition from being brought into England, and Roger performed the ceremony. Lewis now threatened war, and the Pope's advisers urged him to vindicate the rights of Canterbury. Henry was thus driven to a reconciliation, and Thomas returned to his see. He at once suspended the bishops who had taken part in the coronation, renewed the excommunications he had already pronounced against some of them, and excommunicated some of his personal enemies who had annoyed him by violent and brutal acts. The consciousness that he was endangering his own life had no weight with him, for he constantly anticipated and even aspired to martyrdom. When the king, who was still in Normandy, heard of his proceedings he was furiously angry, and thoughtlessly exclaimed to his courtiers, "Of the cowards who eat my bread, is there none that will rid me of this troublesome priest?" Moved by these hasty words, four knights crossed the Channel, proceeded to Canterbury, and after insulting the archbishop in his palace, broke into the church where the monks had compelled him to take shelter. One bade him flee, for else he was a dead man. "I welcome death," he said, "for God and for the liberty of the Church." They tried to lay hands on him, and then the feelings of his younger days, long kept down by self-mortification, asserted themselves. He struggled with the armed men, and threw one to the ground. He cried to another not to dare to touch him, and called him by a foul name. The knights shouted, "Strike! strike!" Then he commended his "soul and the Church's cause to God, to St. Denys of France, to St. Elphege and all the Saints." His murderers attacked him with their swords, and he died with holy words upon his lips. He fell a martyr to the privileges or "liberty" of the Church. That these privileges were not really beneficial to her is not to the purpose. Men and causes are to be judged by the standard of their own age, and neither then nor for centuries later did any doubt that he laid down his life for the cause of God and His Church.

The murder of the archbishop seemed likely to ruin the king. Miracles were worked at the tomb of the martyr, and he was at once accepted as a saint. Although his murder did not cause the revolt that followed it, the disorganization it produced made revolt opportune. Henry's bishops. The only bishop concerned in this movement was Hugh Puiset of Durham, a crafty and powerful prelate, who had some underhand dealings with the Scots, and whose castles were in consequence seized by the king. Henry renounced the Constitutions, promised not to hinder appeals, and submitted to a scourging from the monks of Christ Church. Yet the Church lost much; for the quarrel put an end to the effort to attain to a higher ecclesiastical standard that had been made by Theobald and the clerks of his household, and a fresh wave of secularity swept over the Church. This was largely due to Henry's policy. He kept sees vacant and took their revenues. "Is it not better," he would say, "that the money should be spent on the necessary affairs of the kingdom than on the luxuries of bishops? For the bishops of our time are not like what bishops used to be; they are careless and slothful about their office, and embrace the world with all their arms." He might have made bishops of another stamp, but when, after his absolution, six vacant sees were filled up, he took care that they should go to men who belonged to his own party. Lincoln he gave to his natural son, Geoffrey, who was then a mere lad. The Pope ordered that his consecration should be deferred; yet he held the see, though he was not even a priest, for eight years, until Alexander III. commanded him either to take episcopal orders or to give it up. Then he gave it up, became chancellor, and on his father's death was elected to York. Towards the end of his reign Henry insisted on the election of a bishop of nobler character to the see of Lincoln. This was Hugh of Avalon, the bravest and noblest churchman of his day, whom the king had brought over from Burgundy to govern the little monastery he had founded at Witham, and whom, to his honour, he liked and reverenced. The Lincoln chapter would have preferred a more worldly bishop, and elected several ministers of state and courtiers, one after another. Henry would have none of them; he would not, he said, "for the future, give a bishopric to any one for favour, or relationship, or counsel, or begging, or buying, but only to those whom the Lord should choose for Himself." Canterbury remained vacant for five years after the death of Archbishop Thomas, for some difficulties arose about the election. At last Richard, prior of Dover, was elected. The young King Henry, a worthless man and a rebellious son, affected to be scandalized at his father's interference in episcopal elections, and declared that he managed matters by saying, "I charge you to hold a free election, yet I forbid you to elect any one but my clerk Richard." The archbishop was an easy-going man, and did not please Becket's party. Neither he nor the bishops caused the king any trouble during the remainder of his reign.

His general
relations to
the Church.

Although the Constitutions of Clarendon were nominally abandoned, they had

80

considerable effect on the future relations between Church and State, and indeed determined their development. Even in Henry's reign the privileges which Archbishop Thomas had claimed for the Church were slightly curtailed. With the papal sanction, clerks were made amenable to the forest laws; for what business had they to hunt? And the murderers of clerks were given up to the civil courts; for the claim of the Church to punish them was reduced to an absurdity when it sheltered Becket's murderers from justice, and they were simply punished by such penalties as the Pope, the supreme spiritual judge, could inflict. As Henry caused the lands of the Church, which had hitherto escaped taxation, to bear their share of scutage, so when, for the first time, he introduced a tax on movables the clergy were taxed equally with the laity. This tax, called the Saladine tenth, was granted the king by a great council, and the property both of clerks and laymen was assessed by a jury.

Legates.

After Becket's death Henry took care to keep on good terms with Rome. At his request a legate named Hugh visited this country, partly, at least, to settle a new dispute between Canterbury and York, and from him the king obtained leave to bring the clergy under the forest laws. So far had the martyrdom of St. Thomas injured the independence of the kingdom that even a matter of domestic law was submitted to the papal judgment. Hugh's mission was not successful. At a council held at Westminster in 1176, Roger of York tried to squeeze himself into a more honourable seat than the archbishop of Canterbury. This led to a disturbance in which sticks and fists were freely used. Hugh ran about the chapel in terror, and finding "that he had no authority in England," soon went his way. A few months later Henry showed that, in spite of his late humiliation, he was not prepared to be the Pope's humble servant; for when another legate landed on his way to Scotland, he sent two bishops, who asked him "by whose authority he dared to enter his kingdom without his leave," and exacted a promise from him that he would do nothing here without his will.

Heresy.

Early in the reign we find the spiritual and the secular power acting together in a case that was wholly new to Englishmen. Some thirty German-speaking heretics, probably natives of Flanders, landed here, and made one disciple—a woman. No Christian heretics had ever appeared in England before. Henry summoned a council of bishops to meet at Oxford in 1166; the heretics were found guilty, and were handed over to the "Catholic king." They were condemned to be branded, flogged out of the city, and then to be shunned by all men. Left without food or shelter in the midst of winter, they soon perished. The special action taken with regard to these heretics illustrates the uncertainty of the law as to the punishment of heresy. Here as elsewhere the

Church kept itself free from the pollution of blood, and handed the heretic over to the secular power. Although in the reign of John a clerk who apostatized to Judaism was burnt at Oxford, burning for heresy had no place in the common law of England, except such as was given it by writers of law-books, who were under the influence of the Roman jurisprudence. England was generally free from heresy until the time of Wyclif; the papal Inquisition, though used to some extent for the suppression of the Templars, was not introduced into the kingdom, and the subject of heresy and its punishment is of no practical importance until the appearance of the Lollards.

Conquest of
Ireland.

While the Scottish bishops were, as we have seen, released by the Pope from dependence on the see of York, the influence of the Church of England was extended both in Ireland and Wales. The Church in Ireland seems to have done little to civilize the people: it had lost the early glories of its missionary days, while it retained its lack of order and its inability to rule itself or others. Almost to the eve of the Conquest it had no archbishops, and had a crowd of bishops without a regular diocesan system. These and other irregularities caused some of the bishops of the Ostmen's towns to seek consecration from Lanfranc and Anselm. St. Bernard and Eugenius III. tried hard to introduce some order into the Church, and their efforts were seconded by the Irish bishop, Malachi. Four sees were raised to metropolitan rank, and some steps were taken towards establishing an orderly system. Still, much remained to be done, and Hadrian IV. (Nicolas Brakespear), the only English Pope, willingly sanctioned Henry's proposal to invade Ireland, and in 1155 sent him the bull "Laudabiliter," bidding him conquer the land for the increase of the Church, together with a ring conveying investiture of the country. He did this in virtue of the forged donation of Constantine, which purported to put all islands under the lordship of the Pope. Hadrian's answer to Henry's request was, therefore, a repetition of the answer that Alexander II. made to the request of William. Both Popes alike sanctioned the invasion of a Christian land by a foreign enemy in order to spread the power of the Roman Church. Henry did not take advantage of Hadrian's bull until after the death of Becket. Ireland was conquered by private adventurers, and it only remained for him to receive its submission. He held the land by the Pope's gift, and he was not unmindful of the benefit he had received, for he called together a synod at Cashel, which passed decrees bringing the Church of Ireland into conformity with the Roman order. By far the larger part of the country, however, was virtually unaffected by the Conquest, and equally unaffected by the Council of Cashel. Nor did it become thoroughly papal until Henry VIII. quarrelled with the papacy. Then he disowned the Roman suzerainty by causing himself to be proclaimed king of Ireland, and the papacy appeared as the champion of a country which it had given over to foreign invasion. Unfortunately the bishops that Ireland received from the English kings were often mere ministerial officials, and sometimes little better than the fierce lords of the English Pale.

In Wales, Henry used the Church for political ends, and ruled the country by means of its Norman bishops. The consequence of this policy was, that the bishops were worldly and greedy men, and were hated by the natives, the clergy were ignorant and debased, and the people resisted the claims of the Church. Gerald de Barri, archdeacon of Brecknock, a young man of a noble Norman house, though on his mother's side of the blood-royal of Wales, was appointed by Archbishop Richard as his commissioner to reform the abuses of the Church. He was brave and energetic, very learned and very witty, and most of his books, and especially his "Topography of Ireland" and his "Ecclesiastical Jewel," are delightful reading. While effecting many reforms in the Welsh Church, he seems to have excited the clergy to attempt to gain metropolitan rank for the see of St. David's. This would have been wholly contrary to Henry's policy, for it would have given the Welsh a national leader, and he refused their request. Gerald spent many years of his life, partly in the pursuit of this object, and partly in trying to procure his confirmation as bishop of St. David's. He was twice elected to the bishopric, once in the reign of Henry, and again at the accession of John; he laid his case before Innocent III., and engaged in a long suit at the papal court. St. David's, however, never became a metropolitan see, and he never became its bishop.

Richard's
crusade.

Among the causes that magnified the papal power here and elsewhere must be reckoned the crusades. The Pope alone could release from their vow those who had taken the cross; he became, in a certain sense, the director of the military force of Christendom, and he gained a new claim to interfere in the mutual relations of states. England took little part in the first two crusades, though in Stephen's time our seaport towns joined in a naval crusade of burghers and seamen, who took Lisbon from the Moors. In 1185 the patriarch of Jerusalem urged Henry to come to the help of the Holy city. Two or three barons went to the war, and the king thought of going in person, for he was the head of the Angevin house, to which the kings of Jerusalem belonged. He did not do so, for the same reason which, it is alleged, kept the Confessor from making his proposed pilgrimage. A great council, evidently mainly ecclesiastical in character, reminded him of his coronation oath, and told him that it was his duty to stay and look after the interests of his own kingdom. Two years later Christendom was startled by the news of the fall of Jerusalem. Henry, his son Richard, and many nobles took the cross, and Archbishop Baldwin, accompanied by Gerald de Barri, preached the crusade in Wales, and gained a vast number of recruits. Henry died before he could perform his

84

vow, and Richard immediately began to prepare for his expedition. It was important alike for the good of the kingdom and for his own success that he should decide who should go with him, and accordingly he obtained leave from Clement III. to dispense with crusading vows for money. Before he sailed he sold all the lands, jurisdictions, and offices he could find purchasers for.

William Longchamp, bishop of Ely, 1189-1197.

Richard left the administration in the hands of churchmen, and all through his reign the affairs of the kingdom were managed by bishops. William Longchamp, bishop of Ely, bought the chancellorship; Hugh of Puiset, the justiciarship, and the earldom of Northumberland; and Richard, bishop of London, was treasurer. William Longchamp was a man of low birth, lame and insignificant in person, haughty in manner, of overweening ambition, and careless of the rights of others, active, able, and faithful to his master. Hugh of Puiset, who came of a noble house, was stately and gracious, wary, and full of secular affairs—a rich and powerful prince-bishop. The two ministers soon quarrelled. Bishop William proved the stronger, and put Hugh under arrest. "By the life of my lord," he said, "you shall not go hence till you give me hostages for the surrender of your castles; for I am not a bishop arresting a bishop, but a chancellor arresting his rival." He received a legatine commission, and became sole justiciar. He used his power arrogantly, and so enabled John, the king's brother, to assume the position of a defender of the rights of others. His fall was brought about by an act of violence. Geoffrey, the elect of York, who had met with much opposition from his chapter and from the bishop of Durham, had at last been consecrated in France by the Pope's orders. He now returned to England, in spite, it is said, of having promised the king that he would not do so. An attempt was made to arrest him when he landed at Dover, and he fled to the priory church for refuge. The soldiers of the constable of the castle, the chancellor's brother-in-law, dragged him out of the church by his feet and arms, and he was imprisoned in the castle. There was great indignation at this act. Hugh of Lincoln at once excommunicated the constable and all who had abetted him. Churchmen spoke of Geoffrey as a second St. Thomas, and the lay barons were wroth at the insult put on the son of the late king. All parties united against the chancellor; he was deposed from his office and compelled to leave the kingdom.

Richard was made prisoner as he was returning from the crusade, and his brother John raised a revolt against him. The king committed his interests to

Hubert Walter, bishop of Salisbury. Hubert, as dean of York, had been one of Geoffrey's enemies; he was made bishop by Richard, and accompanied him to Acre, where, we are told, he was equally distinguished as a warrior, a commander, and a pastor. Archbishop Baldwin having died at Acre in 1190, Archbishop Hubert, 1193-1205.the suffragan bishops and the monks of Christ Church, in obedience to the king's will, elected Hubert to the archbishopric in 1193, and shortly afterwards Richard appointed him chief justiciar. A relation of Ralf Glanville, the famous justiciar of Henry II., Hubert had been brought up in a good school for statesmanship, and he did credit to his training. He excommunicated John, took his castles, and ensured his fall by raising the money for the king's ransom. On Richard's return Hubert placed the crown on his head at his second coronation at Winchester, and the king obtained the legatine commission for him. When Richard again left England, Hubert virtually became viceroy of the kingdom. He triumphed over his old enemy, Geoffrey, sent judges to York to decide the dispute between him and his chapter, allowed them to seize the estates of the see, and upheld the cause of the canons, who obtained a papal judgment against their archbishop. Geoffrey left England, and remained abroad for the next five years. During his absence Hubert visited York both as legate and as justiciar.

More honourable to Hubert than this almost personal triumph is his administrative work. Of this it will be sufficient to say here, that he had constantly to find large sums of money for the king; that he did so as far as possible by constitutional methods; that in doing so he accustomed the people to make elections and act by representatives; and that he preserved internal order and developed the constructive work of Henry II. Richard's demands for money were heavy, and though Becket had once opposed Henry on a fiscal question, no constitutional resistance had ever yet been made to a tax proposed by the Crown. Now, however, the nation was to receive from the Church its first lesson in the principle that taxes should only be imposed with the consent of those who have to pay them. Bishop Hugh of Lincoln opposes an unconstitutional tax, 1198.At an assembly held at Oxford in 1198 the archbishop, on the king's behalf, proposed to the barons and bishops that they should maintain three hundred knights for a year to serve across the sea. Then Hugh of Lincoln answered, that though he had come to England as a stranger, he would maintain the rights of his church, and that though it was bound to do military service within the kingdom, the king could not claim such service beyond the sea, and that he would not contribute to a foreign war. Herbert of Salisbury also spoke to the same effect. Their answers naturally appealed to the interests of the lay barons, and the demand was refused, greatly to the king's annoyance.

Hubert's position was not altogether pleasant. The king was always calling on him to find fresh supplies, and he was harassed by a suit brought against him at Rome by his chapter about the college he was building at Lambeth, a subject that belongs to another volume of this series. A serious trouble had also arisen in 1196. The taxes pressed heavily on the lower classes, and a revolt was raised in London, where the richer citizens were accused of throwing the burden of taxation on the poor. The leader of the discontented citizens was a demagogue named William Fitz-Osbert, or William Longbeard, as he was commonly called. Hubert tried to arrest him, but William fled for refuge to the church of St. Mary-le-Bow. By Hubert's order the church was set on fire, and William was smoked out, taken, and hanged. The church belonged to the convent of Christ Church, and the monks, indignant at this breach of sanctuary, complained to Pope Innocent III., who in 1198, wrote to Richard urging him to dismiss his minister, and commanding that for the future bishops and priests should not take part in civil administration. Hubert was therefore compelled to resign the justiciarship.

Much was lost by the absorption of the clergy in secular matters, and St. Hugh did not fail to urge the archbishop to attend less to the affairs of the State and more to those of the Church. The evils that oppressed the Church, the debased lives of the clergy, who generally lived in concubinage, the greediness of the archdeacons and other officials, the worldliness of the bishops, and the venality of the Roman court, are exposed in the satires which bear the name of "Bishop Golias," and are attributed to Walter Map, archdeacon of Oxford. In these poems scarcely a sign appears of any hope of a higher ecclesiastical life; worldliness and evil are represented as triumphant in Christendom. Yet there were some churchmen living noble lives, and the power which St. Hugh exercised in Church and State shows that matters were not past hope. As far as the State was concerned, the employment of the clergy in secular matters was no small gain. Besides providing the country with a succession of highly trained officers, the Church forwarded constitutional development. Just as at first she taught the State how to attain unity, so now she afforded it an example of organization and progress.

CHAPTER VII.

VASSALAGE.

THE ALLIANCE BETWEEN THE
CHURCH AND THE CROWN—
CORONATION OF JOHN—QUARREL
BETWEEN JOHN AND THE POPE—
THE INTERDICT—VASSALAGE OF
ENGLAND—THE GREAT CHARTER
—PAPAL TUTELAGE OF HENRY III.
—TAXATION OF SPIRITUALITIES—
PAPAL OPPRESSION—EDMUND
RICH, ARCHBISHOP—ROBERT
GROSSETESTE, BISHOP OF
LINCOLN—ALIENATION FROM
ROME—CIVIL WAR—INCREASE OF
CLERICAL PRETENSIONS—THE
CANON LAW.

Alliance
between the
Church and
the Crown.

For nearly a century and a half after the Norman Conquest the Church was in
alliance with the Crown. For, though Anselm and Thomas withstood the royal
power when it threatened to overthrow the liberty and privileges of the
Church, and Theobald, Thomas, and Hugh of Lincoln each opposed demands
that seemed to them contrary to right, the bishops generally were staunch
supporters of the Crown, and their alliance helped the king to triumph over
the baronage. This was for the good of the nation at large; for the orderly
though stern despotism of the king was a source of prosperity to the country,
while feudal anarchy entailed general misery and ruin. The strength of the
Crown, and its general alliance with the bishops, enabled it to preserve an
independent attitude towards Rome, and this secured the Church from papal
oppression. Indeed, it was to Rome that churchmen looked for help when the
law of conscience to which they adhered was in danger of being trodden
down by royal power. As long as the king and the Pope had separate interests
the Church was tolerably secure from wrong. In the present chapter we shall
see how the alliance between the Church and the Crown was broken by the
tyranny of John; how the Church, though she gained her rights, was not

content with a selfish victory, and placed herself in the forefront of the battle for national liberty; how the Crown stooped to become the vassal of Rome; and how, throughout the larger part of the long reign of Henry III., the alliance thus formed between the Pope and the king caused the Church to be ground between the upper and nether millstones of royal and papal oppression.

Coronation
of John,
1199.

While the accession of John was strictly in accordance with constitutional usage, it brought the elective character of the monarchy into special prominence; and Archbishop Hubert, at the coronation, while declaring him qualified for election, asserted the freedom of the people's choice, and made a special appeal to John to observe the oath which he had taken. It seems as though, like Dunstan when he crowned Æthelred, he foresaw the consequences of his act, and strove, as the representative of the English Church and people, to impress on the new king the duty he owed to both. Hubert accepted the chancellorship, which was held to be beneath his dignity as archbishop; he used his power to restrain the king from evil, and the hatred that John bore to his memory proves that his death, which took place in 1205, was a national calamity.

Quarrel
between
John and
Innocent
III., 1205.

Before Hubert was buried the younger monks of Christ Church met by night, and without waiting for the king's leave, elected their sub-prior, Reginald, archbishop, and sent him to Rome for confirmation, bidding him tell no one of his new honour. Nevertheless, as soon as he landed in Flanders he gave out that he was archbishop-elect. The king was angry with the convent, for he wished to nominate John de Gray, bishop of Norwich, one of his ministers; the suffragan bishops complained that they had been allowed no share in the election, and the elder and younger monks were opposed to each other. John caused the convent to elect the bishop of Norwich, and gave him the temporalities, and all the parties appealed to Innocent III. After considerable delay—for delays were profitable to the papal court—Innocent declared that the right of election belonged solely to the monks, and that the suffragan bishops had no claim to share in it. He annulled the election of Reginald as altogether illegal, and that of Bishop John, because it was made before the other was declared void; and then, on the ground that the church of Canterbury should no longer be left desolate, commanded the monks, whom

John had sent over to uphold his cause, to elect Stephen Langton, an Englishman, and a cardinal of high position and character. John had given the monks full powers, for he thought that he could trust them, and after a little pressure they yielded to the Pope's command. Innocent wrote to John bidding him receive Stephen. The king answered angrily that he would not do so, that he knew nothing of Stephen save that he had lived among his enemies, that Rome got more out of England than any country on this side the Alps, but that he would narrow the road thither, and that he had plenty of learned prelates in his dominions, and was in no need of sending to a foreigner for judgments. Innocent, who had already shown that he was determined to maintain his authority, as the Vicar of Christ, to judge the kings of the earth, was not to be frightened, and consecrated Stephen Langton. The king turned out the monks of Christ Church, seized the property of the house, and remained obstinate. Meanwhile he quarrelled with the Northern metropolitan also. Many heavy taxes had been laid upon the country, and his brother, Archbishop Geoffrey, refused to allow a new subsidy, demanded from clergy and laity alike, to be levied in his province, and excommunicated the collectors; he appealed to Innocent, but was forced to leave the kingdom, and died abroad.

Interdict,
1208-1213.

When every attempt to persuade John to receive the archbishop had failed, the Pope bade the bishops of London, Ely, and Worcester lay the kingdom under an interdict. No church bells might be rung, no service sung save in low tones, no sacraments administered save confession and the sacrament for the dying, and the dead were buried in unconsecrated ground like dogs, without prayer or priest. In answer, John confiscated all the goods of the clergy and sealed up their barns; the women who lived with them as their wives (*focariæ*) were seized, and they were forced to ransom them, and were ill-used and robbed of their horses as they rode on the highways by the king's men. Several bishops fled the kingdom. This state of things went on for about four years. It was not an unprosperous time with John; he got a great deal of money out of the revenues of the Church and out of the Jews, and made some successful expeditions. At last, in 1212, the Pope published his sentence of special excommunication against him, and absolved his subjects from their allegiance. Men began to say that it was not well to associate with an excommunicated king; and for words like these the archdeacon of Norwich, one of John's fiscal officers, was put to death, partly by starvation, and partly by being weighed down by a massive cloak of lead. Philip II. of France was charged by the Pope to carry out the sentence of deposition, and threatened to invade England.

John

John now found himself in evil case. Wherever he turned there was, or seemed to be, danger; the Welsh rose in rebellion, and word was brought him that his barons, many of whom he had deeply injured, were conspiring against him. Besides, he was much frightened by the prophecy of a certain hermit of Wakefield, who in 1212 declared that on the next Ascension Day he would no longer be king, a prophecy that was repeated from mouth to mouth all through the land. He now gave way entirely; he agreed to receive the archbishop, and to recompense the exiled prelates and the Canterbury monks. On 15th May, 1213, he made submission to the Pope in the person of his legate, a sub-deacon named Pandulf, placed his crown in Pandulf's hands at Dover, did liege homage on receiving it again, and promised the payment of a yearly tribute of 1000 marks for the kingdom of England and the lordship of Ireland. Thus the king of England declared himself the Pope's vassal, and it became the interest of the Pope to uphold his authority. The ecclesiastical difficulty was over, and the victory lay with the Church. Nevertheless the Church, in the person of the primate, now dared to strive against both Pope and king for the liberties of the nation.

The barons, who had stood by quietly while John plundered the Church, felt that it was time to take measures to check his tyranny, for they were disgusted at his pusillanimous submission to the Pope. At a council held at St. Alban's, the justiciar, Geoffrey Fitz-Peter, spoke of the oath the king had taken at his absolution to govern well, and referred to the charter of Henry I. as a standard of good government. He died soon after, and Peter des Roches, bishop of Winchester, a Poitevin, whom John chose as his successor, was no friend to English freedom. The archbishop then came to the front; he held a council of clergy and nobles at St. Paul's, and produced Henry's charter, which seems to have been lost, and had it read before them. The barons were exceeding glad when they heard it, and all took an oath before him that they would fight to the death for the liberties it contained. He promised that he would help them, and so they made a league together. John turned for help to his liege lord, sent a large sum to the Pope, begging him to "confound" the archbishop and excommunicate the barons, and renewed his submission to the papal legate, Nicolas of Tusculum. This Nicolas filled up the many ecclesiastical offices that had fallen vacant during the interdict without regard to the rights of patrons or electors, ordained unfit men, and set at nought the authority of the bishops. They appealed to Innocent, but no good came of it. Meanwhile the northern barons maintained an attitude of opposition to the king, and refused to take part in his war with Philip of France. Moreover, the barons of Poitou would not follow him, his army was defeated at Bouvines, and he came back to England in the autumn of 1214 utterly discredited. During his absence the compensation he had promised had been paid to the bishops and the interdict had been removed, so that his peace with Rome was now firmly secured. On the other hand, the barons, considering that the peace which the king had made with Philip left them exposed to his vengeance, entered into a fresh bond of confederation. Accordingly John endeavoured, with some skill, to divide his enemies, and above all to persuade Stephen Langton to desert the common cause. He issued a charter granting full freedom of election to the Church. When a bishopric or abbacy fell vacant the royal license to elect was to be granted without delay; and if this was not done, the chapter might proceed to make a canonical election without it, and the royal assent was not to be refused unless a sufficient reason could be proved. This was no small boon, for the system of holding elections in the royal court or chapel put the choice of the chapters virtually under the king's control; and as the king received the revenues of vacant bishoprics, it was his interest to prolong the period of vacancy by delays and objections. Nevertheless the archbishop was not to be won over.

The Great
Charter,
1215.

A list of demands, based on the charter of Henry I., and evidently the result of the conferences between the archbishop and the barons, was presented to the king. He asked for time, for he dared not refuse flatly, and pretended that he only wanted to uphold his dignity by appearing to yield of his own will. The archbishop arranged a truce, which John only employed in endeavours to strengthen himself. Stephen Langton therefore gave his full sanction to the assembling of the barons in arms at Stamford in Easter week, 1215, immediately after the conclusion of the truce. John was forced to yield to their demands, and the terms of peace between him and his people form the Great Charter, to which he set his seal at Runnymead on 15th June. On that memorable day the archbishop and several bishops stood by the king as his counsellors, for they had not withdrawn themselves from him, and took no part in the warlike proceedings of the baronial party. Two of them, Peter, the bishop of Winchester, and Walter de Gray, bishop of Worcester, the nephew of John de Gray, for whom the king had tried to gain the primacy, and, like him, one of John's ministers, were decidedly on his side. But the bishops, with Stephen Langton at their head, were as a body in accord with the nation at large in its successful struggle to compel the king to grant this acknowledgment of national liberties. Like the charter of Henry I., the Great

Charter opens with the declaration that the "English Church should be free," and should enjoy its full rights and liberties; and it refers to the special charter on this subject granted the year before. It provides for the rights of all classes, for it bound the barons to extend the same liberties to their tenants that they had obtained from the king; and this and other clauses of general importance are, it is safe to assume, in part at least to be attributed to the influence of the bishops, who thus appear as the champions of the people in the struggle for common rights.

Annulled by
the Pope.

Innocent came to the help of his vassal, and, at John's request, annulled the Charter and pronounced sentence of excommunication against the barons. Peter des Roches and Pandulf were sent to the archbishop to order him to publish this sentence, and on his refusal suspended him. Stephen thereupon left the kingdom and went to Rome. His absence was a great loss to the national party, for the barons held him in awe, and he kept them together. After he left they no longer acted with the same wisdom, unity, or national feeling as before, and a large section joined in inviting Lewis, the eldest son of the French king, to assume the crown. When the archbishop reached Rome his suspension was confirmed by the Pope, and excommunication was pronounced against the barons by name and against the Londoners. This sentence greatly embarrassed the baronial party, though in London it was openly set at nought. The relations between the Pope and the king were fraught with mischief to the Church as well as to the national cause. Besides depriving her of the presence of the primate, Innocent and John combined to confer the see of Norwich on Pandulf, a third-rate papal emissary, who was not even consecrated bishop until about seven years after he had begun to draw the revenues of the bishopric, and never resided in, perhaps never visited, his diocese. And they set at nought the rights of the church of York, which had been left without the presence of an archbishop ever since Geoffrey's departure in 1207. The chapter received leave to elect in 1215, and chose Simon Langton, the brother of the archbishop of Canterbury. John urged the Pope not to confirm the election of the brother of a man who was, he said, his "public enemy," and Innocent accordingly forced the representatives of the chapter to recommend the king's friend, Walter, bishop of Worcester, who received the pall, after binding himself to pay no less than £10,000 to the Roman court for his office. Greatly to the Pope's chagrin, he was unable to prevent Lewis from invading England; and although his legate, Gualo, excommunicated the invader, the king's party dwindled. The tidings of Innocent's death were received in England with joy; he had done all he could to sacrifice the liberties of the nation and the welfare of the Church to the aggrandizement of the papacy, and it was generally believed that his successor, Honorius III., would not follow in his steps. In a few weeks his vassal, John, likewise died.

Papal
tutelage of
Henry III.

Honorius was a wise and careful guardian to the young king, Henry III., and his legate, Gualo, upheld the government of the earl-marshal; the Great Charter was twice reissued, the French were got rid of, and peace was restored. On the other hand, Gualo dealt hardly with the bishops and clergy of the baronial party. He deprived many of the clergy of their benefices and gave them to his own friends; and he compelled the bishops to pay large sums to the Roman court, and to give him considerable gifts also, that they might be allowed to retain their sees. He was succeeded by Pandulf. Stephen Langton had now returned, and was helping Hubert de Burgh to give a thoroughly national character to the administration. The presence of a Roman legate, which had certainly done much, during the early years of the reign, to forward the well-being of the kingdom, became needless. Pandulf was overbearing, and thwarted the archbishop and Hubert. Accordingly the archbishop, who himself had a legatine commission, went to Rome, and obtained a promise from the Pope that no other legate should be appointed as long as he lived, and Pandulf soon afterwards left England. The position of these legates was extraordinary. They controlled the ordinary course of government, directed foreign politics, and continually brought the spiritual power of the papacy to bear on the affairs of the country. Through them their master acted as the guardian of the young king and the suzerain of the kingdom. It is to the credit of Honorius that he willingly brought to a close the period of the tutelage of Henry and of the government of England by foreign legates. From this date the legatine authority of the archbishops of Canterbury was always recognized at Rome, though legates *a latere* were still sent over to England from time to time on special errands.

Henry owed much to the Pope's care, and the gratitude he consequently felt towards the Roman see brought evil on the Church and nation. He became a tool in the hands of successive Popes, who used the wealth of the country for their own purposes. Ecclesiastical preferments were lavishly conferred on Italian adventurers, who were ignorant of the language of the people, and utterly unfit to be their spiritual guides; and the clergy were heavily taxed, sometimes for the Pope's immediate use, and sometimes, by his authority, for the use of the king, though the money thus raised often found its way into the papal treasury. Resistance was difficult, partly because it was widely held that the Pope, as the spiritual father of Christendom, had a right to the goods of the

Church, and partly because, even when the king was angry at the papal demands, the bishops dared not reckon on his support, for his heart was of wax, and never bore the same impression long.

Taxation of
Spiritualities.

The demands made on the clergy in this reign have an important bearing on the history of the Church. Although the movables of the clergy had been taxed for the Saladine tithe and for King Richard's ransom, these were occasions of a special character, and the taxation of spiritualities, or tithes and ings, for national purposes cannot be said to have begun until the Crown and the papacy had become allies. When the Popes demanded money of the clergy for their own use, they did so on the pretext of needing it for the crusades, an object which had an overwhelming claim on Christendom; when they authorized the king to ask for tenths, they acted as protectors of the kingdom. These demands were considered in convocation, and were not granted without the discussion of grievances and petitions for redress. And as the levying of scutage on episcopal lands was an evidence of the right of the bishops to have an equal share with the barons in the deliberations of the great council, so the taxation of clerical movables brought about the secular work of convocation. An example was thus set for the guidance of the future parliament, and the clergy were prepared to take their place as one of the estates of the realm. The payment of tenths to the Pope, while nominally dependent on the consent of the clergy, was virtually compulsory, and was constantly demanded from the middle of this reign. The king did not care to quarrel with the papacy on the matter, and sometimes obtained the papal authority to demand them for his own use.

Papal
oppression.

Among the evils that the Popes brought upon the Church at this period, none were so serious as those that proceeded from their interference with the rights of patronage. This was ordinarily effected by "provisions" or simple announcements that the Pope had provided a person, named or unnamed, for a vacant benefice. The light in which English benefices were regarded at Rome was shown as early as 1226, when Honorius sent a demand, not indeed confined to England, that two prebends in every cathedral church should be made over to the papacy. This demand was rejected by the bishops. While Honorius and his legates did not watch over the young king for nought, the relations between England and the papacy entered on a new and darker phase with the accession of Gregory IX.; for he used this country to supply him with money for his war with the Emperor Frederic II. Moreover, the death of Stephen Langton in 1228 deprived the Church and nation of one of the ablest champions of national rights. Stephen, the papal collector—there was now always an officer of this kind resident in England—roused general indignation by his conduct. He had brought over with him a tribe of usurers, and fear of papal censure drove men to have recourse to them; so the collector and the money-lenders played into one another's hands. The rights of patrons were set aside, and many livings were held by Italians, who never came near them, and farmed them out to others. The wrath of the people broke forth in 1332. A secret league was formed under the direction of a Yorkshire knight, named Robert Twenge, who called himself William Wither. Letters were sent to the bishops and chapters warning them against obeying provisions; and bands of armed knights, with masks on their faces, burst open the granaries of the Italian clerks, distributed their corn among the people, and robbed and beat the foreigners on the highways. Hubert de Burgh, the chief justiciar, was said to have been concerned in the movement, and the accusation hastened his fall. Still, the Pope saw that it was advisable to give way, and sent letters confirming the rights of private patrons. On the death of Stephen Langton the Pope took a further step towards the enslavement of the English Church by treating the course taken by Innocent III. with reference to Langton's election as a precedent for future action. At the request of the king, who offered Gregory the bribe of a tenth on all movables throughout his kingdom, he set aside the choice of the chapter and nominated Richard Grant to the archbishopric.

Edmund
Rich,
archbishop,
1234-1240.

When Richard died in 1234, Gregory confirmed this precedent by quashing three successive elections of the chapter, and compelling the monks to accept Edmund Rich. Edmund had been famous as a teacher at Oxford; he was pious, and had considerable political talent. He saw with indignation the overwhelming influence exercised by the Poitevin and other foreign favourites of the king, against which the bishops as a body were steadily working. He at once took the headship of the national party, and though the Pope favoured the foreigners, compelled the king by a threat of excommunication to dismiss Peter des Roches and his adherents. Nevertheless no permanent reform was effected, and the king's marriage was followed by a fresh influx of foreigners, many of whom were provided for at the expense of the Church. Appeals to Rome were multiplied, and efforts were made to displace the common law for the canon law. Council of Merton, 1236.These efforts caused much displeasure; and when it was proposed at the Council of Merton to bring the law of legitimacy into conformity with the law of Rome, the barons answered, "We will not suffer the laws of England to be changed." The archbishop's authority was weakened by the arrival of the legate Otho, who, in 1237, held a council at London, in which he caused a large body of constitutions to be accepted. Fresh demands were made by Gregory both for money and patronage, and against these the archbishop and clergy protested in vain, for the Pope was upheld by the king. Nevertheless Henry now and then grew restive under the papal yoke, for he knew that he and his kingdom were being ruined, and once, when an unusually large demand was made upon him, told the legate, with oaths and bitter words, that he was sorry he had ever allowed him to land in his kingdom. Edmund found himself set at nought by the legate, thwarted by the king and the Pope, and utterly unable to check the evils by which the Church was oppressed. His troubles reached a climax in 1240, when Gregory, in order to bind the Roman citizens to his side, determined to distribute the benefices of England among their sons and nephews, and ordered the archbishop and two of the bishops to provide benefices for as many as three hundred Roman ecclesiastics. Edmund left the kingdom in despair, and died the same year, and Henry procured the election of Boniface of Savoy, the queen's uncle, a man of worldly mind and small ability, who, though not without some sense of duty, was chiefly guided by his own interests.

Robert
Grosseteste,
bishop of
Lincoln,
1235-1253.

The noblest figure in the history of the Church at this period is that of Robert Grosseteste, bishop of Lincoln, and master of all sciences, as Roger Bacon declared him to be. He was also a man of action; his life was holy and his courage invincible. He was a warm friend of the mendicant friars, the Franciscans and Dominicans, who were established in England in the early part of this reign. The work of these Orders, which will be described in another volume of this series, produced a vast effect on the Church, not merely by moving the laity of every class, especially in towns, to repentance and confession, and by imparting new life to Oxford, but also by stirring up the clergy to efforts after better things. A new light was shining; and children of the light, such as was Robert Grosseteste, were glad to walk in it, while even others were conscious that it would be well to prevent men perceiving that they loved darkness. Grosseteste was anxious for the reformation of his diocese, the largest and most populous in England, and was active in the work of visitation. His canons refused his visitation, and he had a long suit with them, which established the right of bishops to visit their chapters. He endeavoured to enforce celibacy on his clergy, for clerical marriages seem to have been common, and ordered them to prevent excessive drinking and feasting, the practice of sports and plays in churches and churchyards, and all private marriages. He took part in a movement from which the Church still reaps benefit, the erection of vicarages, setting apart in rectories subject to monastic appropriation a sufficient portion of land and tithe for the perpetual and independent endowment of the vicarage. The king sometimes yielded to his influence; but Henry never remained long under one influence, especially if it was for good. Grosseteste always acted under a strong sense of spiritual responsibility; he held that the Pope, when he was in need, had a right to the goods of the clergy, and did not shrink from carrying out his demands. Nor did he raise any objection to the appointment of papal nominees to English benefices on the ground of their foreign birth, or even their ignorance of English. If, however, they were unfit for their duties, either spiritually or canonically, his reverence for the Pope did not blind him, and he refused to present them. Nor did he ever hesitate to resist the king's unrighteous oppression of the Church. Henry's demands on both clergy and laity in 1244 brought about an attempt at combined resistance by the bishops and barons. He met the resistance of the clergy by producing letters from the Pope, Innocent IV., bidding them support his "dearest son." Some of the clergy and laity alike wavered. "Let us not be divided from the common counsel," Grosseteste said, "for it is written, If we are divided we shall all straightway perish." Unfortunately the two orders had not yet learnt the necessity of standing by each other, and the alliance failed.

Extortion
and
remonstrance.

Innocent IV. made at least as large demands on England as Gregory had done, and treated her with more cynical insolence. His envoy, Martin, was like him, and at last goaded the long-suffering nation to violence. Fulk Fitz-Warin came to him with the short message, "Leave England, and begone forthwith." "Who bids me? Did any one send you?" asked the legate. Fulk told him that he was sent by the baronage assembled in arms at a tournament, and warned him that if he delayed to depart till the third day he and all his "would be cut to pieces." The trembling legate complained to the king. Henry, however, told him that he could not restrain his barons. "For the love of God and the reverence of my lord the Pope, give me a safe-conduct!" the legate prayed. "The devil give you a safe-conduct to hell, and all through it!" was the answer of the perplexed and petulant king. A strong remonstrance, in the form of a letter from the people of England, was read by the English representatives at the Council of Lyons, in which it was stated that Italian ecclesiastics drew over 60,000 marks a year from the country. For a while Henry, who was thoroughly alarmed at the state of affairs, wished to check the drain of money to Rome, and wrote to Grosseteste complaining that the bishops had undertaken to collect a tallage which the Pope had laid on the clergy. Grosseteste replied that they were bound to obey their spiritual father and mother (the Pope and the Church) then in exile and suffering persecution, for the papal court was still in exile at Lyons. This view was taken by many noble-minded churchmen, and especially by the friars, who, though they proved themselves the friends of constitutional freedom, strongly maintained the duty of supporting the Popes in their struggle with the Empire.

Henry soon returned to his old relations with the Pope, and matters went from bad to worse. A grant of the tenths of spiritualities was made him by Innocent in 1252. His proctors appeared before an assembly of bishops, and without asking them to allow the tax, proposed its immediate collection. The bishop of Lincoln rose in anger. "What is this, by our Lady?" he said. "You are taking matters for granted. Do you suppose that we will consent to this cursed tax? Let us never bow the knee to Baal." The king tried in vain to frighten some of the bishops by threatening them separately. The next year he obtained a grant, and in return confirmed the Great Charter and the Forest Charter. Special solemnity was given to this act by the bishops. Excommunication was pronounced against all who broke the charters, and when it had been read they dashed the candles which they carried to the ground, saying, "So let those who incur this sentence be quenched and stink in hell;" while the king swore to observe the charters "as a man, a Christian, a knight, a king crowned and anointed." Robert Grosseteste died soon after this ceremony, lamenting with his latest breath the oppressions of the Church, and declaring that her deliverance would only be effected by the sword. Shortly before his death he showed how greatly his feelings had been changed towards the papacy by the troubles that it had brought upon England. Robert Grosseteste's letter to Innocent IV., 1253. Innocent ordered him to induct one of his nephews into a prebendal stall at Lincoln, adding a clause by which the Popes used to override all law—*Non obstante*, any privilege of the church notwithstanding. He refused in a letter in which he speaks plainly of the Pope's conduct, saying that it was not apostolic, and reminding him that there was no sin so hateful to the Lord Jesus Christ as that men should take the milk and the wool of Christ's sheep and betray the flock. When Innocent heard this letter read, he declared that the bishop was a "deaf old dotard," and that his "vassal," the king, ought to imprison him. Here, however, the cardinals interfered, and told the Pope that that might not be, for the bishop was better and holier than any of them, a great philosopher and scholar.

The English
  Church
  alienated
   from
  papacy.

Matters were brought to a crisis by the offer of the crown of Sicily to Henry for his younger son, Edmund, first made by Innocent IV., and confirmed by his successor, Alexander IV., in the hope of using the wealth of England to crush Conrad, and afterwards Manfred, the sons of Frederic II. Henry greedily swallowed the bait, and incurred an enormous debt to the Pope for the war in Apulia. By the advice of Peter, the Provençal bishop of Hereford, he tried to satisfy the Pope by the shameful trick of attaching the seals of the bishops, without their knowledge, to blank bonds, to be filled up as the Pope chose. Alexander IV. treated the English Church as insolently as his predecessor. Soon after the appointment of an Englishman to the deanery of York in 1256, an Italian cardinal appeared in the church, and was installed as dean by his companions; he had been "provided" by the Pope. The archbishop, Sewal de Bovil, had been a pupil of Edmund of Canterbury, by that time canonized, and was a friend of the famous Oxford Franciscan, Adam Marsh. He successfully resisted the intrusion. Death of Sewal de Bovil, archbishop of York, 1258. His courage brought excommunication on him and an interdict on his church, and he died broken-hearted, after sending a letter to the Pope bidding him remember that the Lord's charge to Peter was to "feed His sheep, not shear them or devour them." In 1256, Alexander's envoy, Rustand, pressed the bishops for a tenth for three years for the Sicilian scheme. Fulk, bishop of London, declared that he would sooner lose his head; and Walter of Cantelupe, bishop of Worcester, that he would sooner be hanged. Henry, as his wont was, abused Fulk, and threatened that the Pope should deprive him. "Let them take away my mitre, I shall still keep my helmet," was the bishop's answer. The clergy remonstrated against the envoy's proposal in their diocesan synods, and, thanks to the opposition offered by the lay barons, the Pope and the king were defeated. The reverence which Englishmen formerly had for the Roman Church had now disappeared, and bitter and contemptuous feelings had taken its place. The venality of the papal court and the wrongs of the Church were the favourite themes of the ballad-singer; and English monks loved to tell of visions which represented Innocent as dying struck by the spear of the glorified bishop of Lincoln, and of the sentence pronounced against him by the Eternal Judge on the accusation of the Church he had persecuted and degraded.

The evil and wasteful administration of the king led the barons, in 1258, to place a direct check on the executive, and force Henry to accept the Provisions of Oxford. Simon de Montfort, earl of Leicester, the greatest of the baronial party, had been an intimate friend of Grosseteste, who had consoled and striven to help him in a time of trouble, while Adam Marsh had been his spiritual adviser. Simon was anxious for the welfare of the Church; and the patriotic party among the bishops and the clergy as a body clung steadfastly to him to the last. The national cause, which was already weakened by disunion, received a severe blow in 1261, when the Pope absolved the king from his promises, and annulled the Provisions of Oxford. Two years later the civil war began. After doing all he could to make peace, Walter of Cantelupe threw in his lot with Earl Simon. Before the battle of Lewes, he and Henry, bishop of London, brought to the king the terms offered by the baronial leaders; and when they were rejected, Bishop Walter absolved the barons' soldiers, and exhorted them to quit themselves manfully in the fight. The alliance between the Church and Simon de Montfort is manifest in the legislation that followed the earl's victory: the sphere of ecclesiastical jurisdiction was enlarged, and three bishops were appointed to inquire into grievances. Guido, the legate of Urban, was refused admission into England; he excommunicated the barons, ordered Walter of Cantelupe and other bishops to meet him in France, and sent them back to publish the sentence in England. Their papers were seized and destroyed, probably not against their will, by the people of the Cinque Ports. The next year, when the earl found himself in the power of his foes at Evesham, the aged bishop of Worcester again shrived his host before the battle. After the defeat and death of Simon, Clement IV., the Guido who had been Urban's legate, sent Ottoboni over to England as legate. Ottoboni suspended the five bishops who had upheld the cause of freedom; the bishop of Worcester died the next year, and the others journeyed to Rome, and there purchased their reconciliation. He also did what he could to bring the rebellion to an end by ecclesiastical censures. Peace was completely restored in 1267; the king's elder son, Edward, went on a crusade to Syria, and the Church and the country had a period of rest.

To speak only of the ecclesiastical consequences of the Barons' War, it may be said in a great measure to have reversed the policy of Innocent III., in that it did much towards freeing England from vassalage to the papacy; for the Popes were no longer able to enforce their claim to interfere as suzerains in her affairs. Further, it taught Edward the importance of adopting a national policy, of giving each order in the kingdom a definite place in the constitution, and thus strengthening the national character of the Church; while it also showed him that if he would rule the Church and make its wealth available for his own purposes, he would gain nothing by seeking papal help, and should rather enlist the services of churchmen as his ministers.

Higher idea
of the
clerical
office.

The magnificent pontificate of Innocent III. did not fail to affect the spirit of the English Church and its relations towards the State; it naturally led to a higher idea of the dignity of the clerical office. Partly from this cause, and partly owing to the religious revival effected by the friars, the feeling gathered strength that it was sinful for ecclesiastics to hold secular posts, a point for which Grosseteste contended with much earnestness. With the growth of the papal power there grew up also a desire among the clergy to liberate the administration of ecclesiastical law from the control of secular courts, and the spirit of Innocent may be discerned in Grosseteste's argument, that it was sinful for secular judges to determine whether cases belonged to an ecclesiastical or a secular tribunal. The study of the civil and canon laws was eagerly pursued; it was stimulated by the influence of the large number of foreign ecclesiastics, and even common lawyers found in it a scientific basis for their own law. Rival systems of law. Clerical jurists were naturally aggressive, and the party devoted to the increase of clerical dignity and power strove to displace the national by the foreign system. The nation at large, hating the foreigners who preyed upon the country, was strongly opposed to the introduction of foreign law, and this opposition prompted the reply of the barons to the proposal made at Merton in 1236, when an attempt was made to change the law of England, which was, on the point in question, held by Grosseteste and the clergy generally to be sinful, and to bring it into accordance with the law of Rome. And the same feeling had led, not long before, to the compulsory closing of the schools of civil and canon law in London. On the other hand, the authority of these laws was upheld by the policy of Gregory IX. A code of papal decrees was compiled with his sanction, and he was anxious to procure its acceptance throughout Latin Christendom. What may almost be described as a corresponding step was taken in England by the publication of a series of constitutions which formed the foundation of our national canon law—the constitutions of Stephen Langton, of the legates Otho and Ottoboni, of Boniface of Savoy, and other archbishops. In some of these a considerable advance in the pretensions of the clergy is evident. The work of Edward I. in assigning the clerical estate its place in the scheme of national government, in forcing it to bear its own (often an unduly large) share in the national burdens, and in limiting and defining the area of clerical jurisdiction and lawful pretensions so as to prevent them from trenching on the national system, will form the main subject of the next chapter.

CHAPTER VIII.

THE CHURCH AND THE NATION.

Edward I.,
1272-1307.

In the reign of Edward I. the relations between the Church and the Crown were defined and settled on a constitutional basis, and the clergy were assigned their own place in the national system. The king was a great lawgiver, and out of a chaotic mass of customs and institutions chose those best adapted to create an orderly polity, in which every class of men fitted for political purposes had its own share both of rights and duties. At the same time, he had no intention of giving up any of the prerogatives of the Crown, for he both loved power for its own sake and was in constant need of money. His reign was, therefore, full of struggles with those to whom he was giving ascertained rights to share in the government. He met with considerable opposition from the clergy, for the influence of the mendicant revival was directed to uphold the papal pretensions, and as far as possible to render the Church independent of the State. The main history of his struggles with the clergy assumes two distinct phases during the periods of the archiepiscopates of Peckham and Winchelsey. Peckham contended chiefly for the privileges of the National Church; and the king, who still remained in accord with Rome, got the better of him, and prevented clerical privilege from hindering his scheme of national government. Fortunately for the Church and the nation, the hold of the Pope upon the country was loosened by the breach of the accord between the papacy and the Crown which had existed ever since the submission of John. This breach was brought about by the extravagant pretensions of Rome. During the latter part of the reign, Winchelsey endeavoured to uphold these pretensions, as he was to some extent bound to do by his office. He did not, however, confine himself, as Peckham had done, simply to an ecclesiastical policy; for he took a leading part in various attempts to diminish the power of the Crown, and sought to secure a separate position for the Church, with the Pope instead of the king as her ruler, by allying himself with the party of opposition. Edward was forced to yield to the political demands made upon him; but he successfully maintained the rights of the Crown over the Church, and punished the archbishop for the part he had taken against him. The clergy equally with the laity had to bear their share of the national burdens; the claims of Rome were defeated, and the parliament set out on the course of resistance to the papal usurpations which found its completion in the sixteenth century.

During the early years of Edward's reign matters went on smoothly between the Church and the Crown. Gregory X. was the king's friend, and had accompanied him on his crusade; and his chief adviser and chancellor was Robert Burnell, a churchman of great ability and wisdom, who thoroughly understood how to forward his master's ecclesiastical policy. Before Edward became king he had endeavoured to prevail on the monks of Christ Church to elect Burnell to succeed Archbishop Boniface. Archbishop Kilwardby, 1273; res. 1278.Nevertheless they chose another as archbishop; the king refused his assent to the election, and Gregory, to put an end to the vacancy, appointed Robert Kilwardby, a Dominican friar. Kilwardby, however, was by no means sufficiently vigorous in asserting the rights of the Church to satisfy Nicolas III., and allowed the privileges of the clergy in matters of jurisdiction to be curtailed by statute. Nicolas accordingly raised him to the cardinalate in 1278, called him to Rome, and thus forced him to resign the archbishopric. Edward secured the election of his friend and minister, Burnell, then bishop of Bath and Wells, and urged the Pope to confirm it. Archbishop Peckham, 1279-1292.He was again foiled; for Nicolas, after causing inquiries to be made as to the fitness of the archbishop-elect, informed the king that he could not assent to his request, and appointed John Peckham, the provincial of the English Franciscans, laying down the rule that, as the death of a prelate at Rome had long been held to give the Pope the right of appointing a successor, a resignation, which was, he declared, an analogous event, had the same effect.

Robert Burnell and the new archbishop were extreme types of two opposite sorts of churchmen. The chancellor, who was wholly devoted to the king's service, was a statesman of high order. He was magnificent in his tastes and expenditure, held many rich preferments, and took care that his relations also should be enriched out of the wealth of the Church. His mode of life was secular, and the grand matches that he arranged for his daughters created no small scandal. Peckham, on the other hand, was a model friar, pious and learned, with exalted ideas of the rights of the papacy and the privileges of the clergy. He was fearless and conscientious, unwise and impracticable. Between him and Bishop Robert and the other clerical advisers of the king there was, of course, no sympathy. He was anxious that the dignities and benefices of the Church should be worthily bestowed, and laboured to carry out the injunctions of Nicolas III. against the prevalent abuse of pluralities. On this matter Peckham wrote plainly to Edward that he would oblige him as far as he might without offending God, but could go no further, and that he was already sneered at for "conniving at the damnable multitude of benefices held by his clerks." Nicolas strove to check the promotion of secular-minded bishops, and when Edward procured the election of Burnell to the see of Winchester, ordered the chapter to proceed to another election. Peckham was blamed for this, and it was also alleged that he had used his influence at Rome against another of the king's ministers, Anthony Bek, afterwards the warlike bishop of Durham. However, he denied that he had said anything to hinder the promotion of either.

Almost immediately on his arrival in England in 1279, the archbishop came into collision with the king. He held a provincial council at Reading, in which, besides publishing the canons of the Council of Lyons against pluralities, he decreed that excommunication should be pronounced against all who obtained the king's writ to stop proceedings in ecclesiastical suits against any royal officer who refused to carry out the sentence of a spiritual court, and against all who impugned the Great Charter; and further ordered that the clergy should expound these decrees to their parishioners, and affix copies of the Charter to the doors of cathedral and collegiate churches. These decrees were a direct challenge to the king, and Edward treated them as such; for in his next parliament he compelled Peckham to revoke them, and to declare that nothing that had been done at the council should be held to prejudice the rights of the Crown or the kingdom.

Statute of
Mortmain,
1279.

106

Edward further rebuffed the archbishop by publishing the statute "De Religiosis" or "of Mortmain." This statute, though, as regards the date of its promulgation part of Edward's answer to Peckham's assumption, was directed against an abuse of long standing, and was in strict accordance with the king's general policy. It forbade, on pain of forfeiture, the alienation of land to religious bodies which were incapable of performing the services due from it. Land so conveyed was said to be in *mortmain*, or in a dead hand, because it no longer yielded profit to the lord, who was thus defrauded of his right of service, escheat, and other feudal incidents. Besides the vast amount of land that was held by the Church, estates were often fraudulently conveyed to ecclesiastical bodies, to be received again free of services by the alienor as tenant; and thus the superior lord, and the king as capital lord, were cheated, and the means for the defence of the realm were diminished. These evils were partially checked by Henry II., who levied scutage on the knights' fees held by the clergy, and the practice of conveying lands in mortmain was prohibited by one of the Provisions of Westminster in 1259. Edward's statute gave force to this provision by rendering it lawful, in case the immediate lord neglected to avail himself of the forfeiture, for the next chief lord to do so. Moreover, the king still further showed his discontent at the attitude of the clergy by demanding an aid from them. In spite of these rebuffs, Peckham pursued his policy of attempting to enlarge the sphere of spiritual jurisdiction at the cost of the jurisdiction of the Crown, and proposals were made in a council which he held at Lambeth in 1281 to remove suits concerning patronage and the goods of the clergy from the royal to the ecclesiastical courts. Here, however, the king interfered, and peremptorily forbade the council to meddle in matters affecting the Crown. Peckham was forced to give way, and shortly afterwards sent Edward a letter asserting in the strongest terms the liberties of the Church as agreeable to Scripture and the history of England, pointing out that it was his duty to order his conduct by the decrees of the Popes and the rules of the Church, referring the oppressions under which, he said, the clergy were suffering to the policy of Henry I. and Henry II., and reminding the king of the martyrdom of St. Thomas of Canterbury for the Church's sake.

Conquest of
  Wales,
  1282.

When Edward invaded Wales in 1282, Peckham, moved with a desire for peace and with compassion for the Welsh, endeavoured to persuade Llewelyn to submit to the English king, and, contrary to Edward's will, went alone to Llewelyn's fortress of Aber, and tried to arrange terms. When his efforts proved in vain, he wrote an angry and irritating letter to the Welsh prince. Nevertheless he exerted himself on behalf of the Welsh clergy, prayed Edward to allow the clerks in Snowdon to leave the country with their goods, wrote indignantly to Burnell to complain that some clerks had been hanged at Rhuddlan, "to the reproach of the clergy and the contempt of the Church," and exhorted the king to restore the churches that had been destroyed in the war. The backward and disorderly condition of the Welsh Church caused him much concern, and he urged the bishops of Bangor and St. Asaph's to put a stop to the concubinage or marriage of the clergy, their unseemly dress, and their neglect of their duties, to insist on the observance of the decrees of Otho and Ottoboni, and to do all in their power to overcome the angry feelings of their flocks towards the English, so that the very word "foreignry" might no more be used among them. Moreover, he was anxious to see the Welsh become civilized, and wrote to Edward advising him to encourage them to settle in towns and follow industries, and, as there were no means of education in Wales, to make the Welsh boys come to England and be taught there, instead of entering the household of a native prince, where they learnt nothing but robbery. Indeed, it would have been well for Wales had Peckham's wishes on these and other matters been carried out. The war taxed the king's resources severely, and, towards the end of it, Edward ordered the seizure of the money that, in accordance with a decree of the Council of Lyons, had been collected for a crusade, and stored in various great churches in England. This brought an indignant letter from Pope Martin IV. Before its arrival, however, the king had promised that the money should be refunded. Not content with a promise, the archbishop went off to meet Edward at Acton Burnell, and prevailed on him to make immediate restitution.

Limits of
spiritual
jurisdiction
defined.

Undismayed by his previous failures, Peckham, in 1285, made another attempt to secure the independence of the Church in matters of jurisdiction; and a series of articles was drawn up by the bishops of his province in convocation, and presented to the king. The most important of these urged that a check should be put on the issue of prohibitions from the king's court staying proceedings in ecclesiastical courts. The articles were answered by the chancellor; some concessions were made which failed to satisfy the bishops, and a reply was sent criticizing the chancellor's answers. Edward was determined to settle the relations of the Church and the Crown in these matters. He had, perhaps before receiving the articles, caused an inquisition to be made into suits brought by the clergy against laymen, had imprisoned all the judges and officers of the ecclesiastical courts who were convicted of having fined laymen too heavily, and had declared that these courts could not claim as of right the cognizance of any save matrimonial and testamentary causes. This violent curtailment of the rights of the Church was maintained during the dispute with the prelates. It was modified shortly afterwards by a writ, addressed to the bishops by the king in parliament, and called "Circumspecte agatis." By this writ, which had the force of a statute, ecclesiastical jurisdiction was defined as extending to cases of deadly sin which were visited by penance or fine, and offences as regards things spiritual, such as neglect of churches, to suits about tithes and offerings, assaults on clerks, defamation, and perjury which did not involve a question of money. This writ, then, ascertained the limits between the areas proper to the secular and the ecclesiastical courts, settled the relations between Church and State in England as far as jurisdiction was concerned, and declared the triumph of the principles which Henry II. had laid down in the Constitutions of Clarendon. The punishments inflicted by spiritual judges for the correction of the soul put a salutary check on violence and debauchery; and if sometimes the clergy used their spiritual power to defend their temporal rights, they executed justice on offenders against morality without respect of persons. Peckham gave a signal instance of this by condemning Sir Osbert Giffard, who had carried off two nuns from Wilton, to nine public floggings, to fasting, and to put off the dress and accoutrements of a knight and a gentleman until he had made a three years' pilgrimage to the Holy Land. And as an ecclesiastical judge had a right to a writ committing any excommunicated person to prison until satisfaction was given to the Church, an offender was forced to submit to the penance imposed on him.

Expulsion
of the Jews,
1290.

Although the expulsion of the Jews is chiefly a matter of economic and constitutional importance, it has also an ecclesiastical bearing. In spite of Edward's policy in Church matters, he was a religious man. When he was in trouble or danger he made vows which he always performed: he often passed Lent to some extent in retirement, and he seems to have been pleased to attend religious ceremonies. Apart, therefore, from worldly reasons, he must have felt—for such was the general feeling of the day—that the protection afforded to the Jews by the Crown and the profit they brought to the Exchequer were alike ungodly. Besides, as a crusader he was bound to hate the enemies of the cross. The Jews were wealthy, and did no small harm by their usurious practices. Although Edward forbade them to carry on usury, the law does not seem to have been enforced; and the rich, and among them even the excellent Queen Eleanor, profited by their extortions. While the king treated them with much severity, he seems to have been anxious for their conversion, though the means adopted to bring this about were not always judicious. They were compelled to attend and listen diligently to sermons preached against their faith; the Converts' House in London was re-endowed, and Peckham was careful to prevent them from building any new synagogues in the city. Edward, who, soon after he had taken a second crusading vow in 1287, had ordered the Jews to leave his continental dominions, at last, in 1290, greatly to the delight of all classes, expelled them from England. Both clergy and laity testified their approval of the measure by making him a grant.

Clerical
taxation.

During the early part of Edward's reign, the clergy had no reason to complain of excessive taxation. Some discontent was, indeed, felt at the new and more stringent valuation of clerical property which was made after Nicolas IV. had, in 1288, granted the king a tenth for six years for the purpose of a new crusade. This valuation, called the "Taxation of Pope Nicolas," took cognizance of both the temporalities and the spiritualities of the clergy, and was used as the basis for ecclesiastical taxation until the sixteenth century. In 1294, however, Edward was in great straits for money, for he was forced into a war with France. Robert Burnell was dead, and the measures Edward adopted to raise money probably show how much he lost by his minister's death. Among other unconstitutional acts, he seized the money and treasure stored in the cathedrals and abbeys. He called an assembly of the clergy of both provinces and demanded a grant. Archbishop Winchelsey, 1294-1313. The clergy had no head; for Peckham died in 1292, and Robert Winchelsey, who had been elected as his successor, was still at Rome, whither he had gone for consecration. They failed to appreciate the urgency of the crisis, and offered a single grant of two-tenths. Edward was indignant, and declared that they should give him one-half of their revenues, or he would outlaw them. The dean of St. Paul's, who went to court hoping to pacify him, was so frightened at his anger that he fell down dead. Finally, Edward sent a knight to the assembled clergy; his messenger bluntly stated the king's demand, and added, "Whoever of you will say him nay, let him stand up that he may be known." They tried to make conditions, and prayed for the abrogation of the Statute of Mortmain. To this the king would not consent, and they were forced to yield to his grievous demand.

Parliamentary
representation.

Edward's need of money led him to perfect the organization of parliament as an assembly of estates competent to speak and act for the nation. In this assembly the estate of the clergy was to have its place. National councils of the Church, though held on the occasion of legatine visits, consisted only of bishops, and had fallen into disuse; and the clerical grants were made by the convocations of the two provinces separately. Besides these provincial convocations, the clergy met in diocesan synods, and also in assemblies of archdeaconries or other districts. The diocesan synods, the cathedral chapters, and sometimes the smaller clerical assemblies, were consulted as to proposed grants, and acted independently of each other. In the last reign, for example, the rectors of Berkshire drew up a remonstrance against a grant to help the Pope in his war with the Emperor. Inconvenient as it was, the practice of seeking the assent of local synods to taxation was necessary so long as the whole body of the beneficed clergy was not systematically represented in convocation. The principle of clerical representation had gained ground during the reign of Henry III., and in 1283 Peckham confirmed it by fixing the manner in which it was to be carried out. Two proctors were to be chosen by the clergy of each diocese of the southern province, and one for each cathedral and collegiate chapter. In the northern province the custom of choosing two proctors for each archdeaconry appears to have obtained somewhat earlier. Edward, when settling the representation of the clergy in Parliament, adopted Peckham's system, and in summoning the bishops to the parliament of 1295, which has served as a model for all future parliaments, caused a clause, called the "*præmunientes*" clause, to be inserted in the writs, directing each bishop to order the election of two proctors for the clergy of his diocese and one for his cathedral chapter, who should attend parliament with full power to "discuss, ordain, and act." Thus the clergy became one of the parliamentary estates, and, like the other estates, made their grants independently, and possibly deliberated apart. As, however, their tendency was at this time towards the assertion of a separate position in the State, they did not value this change, and, as we shall see, soon succeeded in establishing the custom of making their grants in their own convocations.

Breach
between the
Crown and
the Papacy.

The submission of John to Innocent III. had established an accord between the Crown and the papacy that had in the last reign been fraught with evil to the Church. It came to an end because Edward, who was determined that the Church should be national in the fullest sense, and should take its place in the national system with clearly defined rights and with a liability to public burdens, found his plans opposed by a Pope who would recognize no limit to his authority, or to the immunities of the clergy. This Pope was Boniface VIII. Forgetful alike of the spirit of resistance to papal interference that had lately been exhibited in England, of the increase of independent thought that had arisen from the influence of the universities, and of the effect of the doctrines of the civil lawyers in magnifying the authority of the king, and equally forgetful of the rapid advance of the power of the French monarchy, Boniface attempted to usurp the rights of the Crown in both countries. In February

1296 he published the bull "Clercis laicos," forbidding, on pain of excommunication, the clergy to grant, or the secular power to take, any taxes from the revenues of churches or the goods of clerks. In the October parliament the laity made their grants; but the clergy, after a debate led by Winchelsey, which lasted several days, informed the king that they could grant him nothing. Edward would not accept this answer, and ordered Winchelsey to let him know their final determination the following January. The archbishop accordingly held a convocation at St. Paul's on St. Hilary's Day, to decide whether there was any middle way between disobeying the Pope and disobeying the king. Hugh Despenser and a clerk, who attended as the king's proctors, set forth the dangers of foreign invasion that threatened the kingdom. By way of reply, Winchelsey caused the Pope's bull to be read. Despenser then plainly told the clergy that unless they granted the sum needed for the defence of the country the king and the lords would treat their revenues as might seem good to them. They persevered in their refusal; and on the 12th of February the king, who was in urgent need of supplies for the war against France, outlawed the whole of the clergy of the southern province, took their lay fees into his own hand, and allowed any one who would to seize their horses. Meanwhile Winchelsey excommunicated all who should contravene the papal decree. The clergy of the northern province, however, submitted, and received letters of protection. Edward's difficulties were increased by the refusal of his lords, led by the Constable and Marshal, the Earls Bohun and Bigod, to make an expedition to Flanders whilst he went to the army in Gascony. Winchelsey, though not wavering himself, was unwilling to expose any of his clergy to further danger, if they could find a way of escape, and held another convocation, in which he bade each "save his own soul." Many of them accordingly compounded with the commissioners whom the king had appointed for that purpose.

Winchelsey
  and the
  Charters.

In spite of the threatening attitude of the malcontent lords, Edward could not refuse to fulfil his engagements to his allies. He raised supplies and a force by means which, though unconstitutional, were justified by necessity, was reconciled to the archbishop, and took a solemn leave of his people from a platform in front of Westminster Hall, telling them that he knew that he had not reigned as well as he ought, but that all the money that had been taken from them had been spent in their defence, and requesting them, if he did not return from Flanders, to crown his son Edward. Winchelsey wept at the king's words, and all the people shouted assent. Nevertheless, the barons remained rebellious, demanded that the king should confirm the Great Charter and the Forest Charter, and presented a petition of grievances. Nor was the

112

ecclesiastical matter settled, though the clergy offered to ask the Pope's leave to make a grant. Before Edward left he taxed the temporalities of the clergy, for he evidently suspected them of acting with the malcontents. Soon after he had set sail, the barons came up armed to a council at London, which was attended by the bishops, though not by the inferior clergy. Winchelsey seems to have presided at this council; and apparently by his advice the young Edward, whom his father had left as regent, was required to confirm the charters with certain additions. He assented, and sent the charters to his father, who confirmed them along with the new articles. These articles may be said to have declared it illegal for the Crown to levy any taxes or imposts, save those anciently pertaining to it, without the consent of parliament.

In November the ecclesiastical dispute was brought to an end. Early in the year Boniface, to satisfy Philip of France, declared that he did not forbid the clergy to contribute to national defence or to make voluntary grants; and Winchelsey took advantage of a Scottish invasion to recommend the clergy to tax themselves. The dispute had been independent of the rebellious behaviour of the Constable and Marshal, who had taken advantage of it to put pressure on the king. Winchelsey's conduct with regard to the proceedings of the earls seems to prove that he had an enlightened desire for constitutional freedom; and the Church in his person again appeared, as she had appeared so often before, as the assertor of national rights. Nor did the Church fail to gain much by the issue of the ecclesiastical dispute. The victory lay with the Crown; the national character of the Church was established, and it was saved from the danger of sinking into a handmaid of Rome, which would probably have come to pass if the papacy and the Crown had remained at one. From henceforth the Church generally found the State ready to protect her liberties from papal invasion.

Winchelsey's
   policy of
 opposition.

After Edward's return fresh demands were made upon him, and a long struggle ensued between him and the parliament on the subject of disafforestation, or the reduction of the royal forests to their ancient boundaries. Winchelsey evidently continued in opposition, partly with the view of increasing the papal authority by embarrassing the king. His desire to uphold the Pope's authority led him at last to commit the fatal error of opposing a cause of national concern. Edward's claim to the crown of Scotland was alternately admitted and rejected by the Scottish lords, who submitted to him when he overawed them by appearing in Scotland at the head of his forces, and rebelled when he returned to England. Finding themselves unable to resist him, they appealed to Boniface to help them.

Accordingly, in 1299, Boniface published a bull asserting that the kingdom of Scotland was a fief of the Holy See, and ordering Edward to submit his claim to the decision of Rome. On receiving this bull Winchelsey journeyed to Galloway, where Edward then was, and in August 1300 appeared before him, in company with a papal envoy, presented the bull, and added, it is said, an exhortation of his own on the duty of obedience and the happiness of those who were as the people of Jerusalem and as Mount Zion. "By God's blood!" shouted the indignant king, "I will not hold my peace for Zion, nor keep silence for Jerusalem, but will defend my right that is known to all the world with all my might." The archbishop was bidden to inform the Pope that the king would send him an answer after he had consulted with his lords, for "it was the custom of England that in matters touching the state of the realm all those who were affected by the business should be consulted."

Acting on this principle, Edward, early the next year, laid the bull before his barons at a parliament held at Lincoln, and bade them proceed in the matter. Accordingly they wrote to the Pope, on behalf of themselves and the whole community of the realm, briefly informing him that the feudal superiority over Scotland belonged to the English Crown; that the kings of England ought not to answer before any judge, ecclesiastical or secular, concerning their rights in that kingdom; that they had determined that their king should not answer concerning them or any other of his temporal rights before the Pope, or accept his judgment, or send proctors to his court; and that, even if he were willing to obey the bull, they would not allow him to do so. This letter was signed by the lay baronage only, not by the bishops. At this parliament the barons requested the king to dismiss his treasurer, Walter Langton, bishop of Lichfield, and presented certain petitions for reform. Most of these petitions were granted, and among them the demand for disafforestation; the last, that the goods of the clergy should not be taxed against the will of the Pope, evidently bears witness to the terms of the alliance between Winchelsey and the barons. This article was rejected by the king, who thus further separated the baronial from the clerical interest. Nor did he dismiss Langton, who was soon afterwards suspended from his bishopric on charges of adultery, simony, homicide, and dealings with the devil; he was acquitted by the Pope, and probably owed his suspension to Winchelsey's enmity.

Clement V.,
1305-1316.

The overthrow of Boniface by the French king, Philip IV., involved the failure of his attempt to establish the dominion of the papacy over national churches. Clement V., the next Pope but one, was a Gascon, and settled the papal court at Avignon, where it remained for seventy years, a period called the "Babylonish captivity." During this period the papal court became a French

114

institution. This caused Englishmen to be very jealous of the Pope's interference; and when the king was at one with his people the Popes were not allowed to exercise much authority here, and the national character of the Church was effectually defended. Clement was anxious to oblige Edward. As a Gascon noble, and as archbishop of Bordeaux, he had been his subject, and as Pope he was not willing to become the tool of the French king. Edward took advantage of his goodwill. He considered that his people had dealt hardly with him, and had forced him to give up his just rights, and he obtained a bull from the Pope absolving him from the oaths which he had taken. In doing so he simply acted in accordance with the ideas of his time, and this is the one excuse that can be made for him. Nor was he content with thus providing for the repair of his royal dignity; he took vengeance on the man who had done as much as any one to lessen it. Winchelsey suspended.In 1305, when the old baronial opposition had wholly ceased, he accused Winchelsey of having engaged in treason in 1301, and added other causes of complaint against him. Edward submitted the charges against him to the Pope, who suspended him, and summoned him to Rome. He did not return to England until after the king's death. Although the Pope took the administration of the see of Canterbury into his own hands, the king, of course, seized the temporalities. Clement complained of this; and Edward, in order to ensure the continuance of his triumph over the archbishop, allowed the Pope's agents to receive the profits arising from them.

While, however, the king and the Pope were thus obliging one another, the papacy had nevertheless lost ground in England. For full eighty years its power here had depended mainly on its alliance with the Crown; and now that Boniface had shown that this power, if unchecked, would destroy the rights of the Crown over the Church, the king was prepared to join with his people in resisting it. Remonstrance of parliament against papal exactions, 1307.Winchelsey's absence afforded an opportunity. In a parliament held at Carlisle in 1307, statutes were published prohibiting the taxation of English monasteries by their foreign superiors; and while much debate was being held on the oppression of Rome, a letter was found, written under an assumed name and addressed to the "Noble Church of England, now in mire and servitude," which set forth in terms of bitter sarcasm the evils she suffered from her "pretended father" the Pope. This letter was read before the king, a cardinal-legate who was visiting England to arrange the marriage of the Prince of Wales, and the whole parliament. A document was then drawn up enumerating the encroachments of Rome which were carried out by the papal agents and collectors. These were the appointment of foreigners to English benefices by provisions; the application of monastic revenues to the maintenance of cardinals; the reservation of first-fruits, then a novel claim; the increase in the amount demanded as Peter's pence, and other oppressions. The cause of complaint with reference to Peter's pence arose from an attempt of William de Testa, the Pope's collector, to demand a penny for each household, instead of the fixed sum hitherto paid. The articles were accepted and forwarded to the Pope, and Testa was examined before parliament, and ordered to abstain from further exactions. Edward, however, was hampered by his need of Clement's co-operation. After the parliament was dissolved, he was persuaded by the cardinal to allow Testa to proceed with the collection of first-fruits; and when the papal agents appeared before the council to answer the charges made against them in parliament, they took up an aggressive position, and complained that they had been hindered in the execution of their duty. Before these matters were brought to a conclusion the king died.

Edward II.,
1307-1327.

Immediately on his accession, Edward II. recalled Winchelsey, and imprisoned his father's minister, Walter Langton. The resistance to papal exactions was renewed in a parliament held at Stamford in 1309, where the king gave his consent to a petition presented by the lay estates for the reformation of civil abuses. At this parliament the barons sent a letter of complaint to the Pope of much the same character as the document drawn up at Carlisle. Clement, by way of answer, complained that his collectors were impeded, that his briefs and citations were not respected, that laymen exercised jurisdiction over spiritual persons, and that the tribute granted by John to the See of Rome had not been paid for some fifteen years. Here the matter seems to have ended, and the chief features of our Church history during this wretched reign are closely connected with the quarrels and general disorganization that prevailed in the kingdom. For a time Winchelsey acted with the king, but Edward's carelessness and evil government drove him into opposition. While the country at large had much to complain of, the Church had her special grievances. In 1309 the archbishop held a provincial council to decide on proceedings against the Templars; for the king had promised the Pope that the English Church should take part in attacking the Order. At this council gravamina were adopted which show that constant encroachments were made on the sphere of ecclesiastical jurisdiction. The next year the archbishop and six of his suffragans were chosen as "Ordainers," the name given to a commission appointed by a council of magnates, lay and spiritual, to carry out a system of reform. Winchelsey and the bishops of his province pronounced excommunication against all who hindered the ordinances, or revealed the secrets of the Ordainers. First among the objects which the Ordainers swore to promote was the increase of the honour and welfare of the Church; and the interference with the spiritual courts which had been complained of the year before was forbidden by one of their ordinances. As Winchelsey thus joined the party of opposition, the king, in 1312, released Langton, and appointed him treasurer; for, in spite of all that had passed, the old servant of Edward I. upheld the cause of the Crown. The earl of Lancaster, the head of the opposition, seems to have been regarded as favourable to the claims of the Church; for in 1316, when he had virtually obtained the complete control of the kingdom, the estate of the clergy presented, in a parliament held at Lincoln, a series of complaints called "Articuli Cleri." The royal assent was given, and the "articles" became a statute. By these articles the rules laid down in the writ "Circumspecte agatis" were re-enacted, and various rights and liberties, touching matters of jurisdiction and sanctuary, were acknowledged. Among these, it was allowed that it pertained to a spiritual, and not to any temporal judge, to examine into the fitness of a parson presented to a benefice, and that elections to dignities should be free from lay interference.

Bishops
appointed
by
provision.

Throughout the whole reign elections by capitular bodies were constantly set at nought. Sometimes the Pope appointed to a bishopric on the king's recommendation, and sometimes in spite of his wishes. From the time of Stephen Langton onwards, the Popes had so often interfered with the appointment to the primacy, either, as in the case of Peckham, acting in opposition to the Crown, or, as in that of Winchelsey, in unison with it, that their claim was now tacitly admitted. As regards suffragan bishoprics, their interference was often exercised owing either to the death of a bishop at Rome, or to appeals. Besides, it seems to have been laid down in this reign that the right of appointing to a see vacant by translation belonged to the Pope, who alone had the power to sanction the divorce between a bishop and his diocese. The embarrassments of Edward II. encouraged a still greater encroachment on the rights of the Church and of the Crown; and Clement simply appointed bishops by reservation and provision, declaring that he had during the lifetime of the last bishop reserved the appointment for himself, and that as a vacancy had occurred, he had found a fit man, and provided him accordingly. In some cases the bishop thus provided had been nominated by the Crown and elected by the chapter; in others the wishes of both were set aside out of the fulness of the Pope's power.

The bishops of this reign were as a body, though with some exceptions, worldly and self-seeking. On the death of Winchelsey, in 1313, the monks of Christ Church chose a new archbishop of high repute for learning and character. At the king's request, Clement set aside their election and appointed Edward's old tutor, Walter Reynolds, bishop of Worcester, the son of a baker, and a man in all respects unworthy of such an office. Before he came to the throne Edward had found him useful to him, and when he became king he made him treasurer and chancellor. During the troubles of the reign, Reynolds adhered to the king until he began to suspect that it was no longer his interest to do so. An election made by the chapter of Durham was set aside by John XXII., who provided Lewis Beaumont, an ignorant man, and lame in both his feet, so that it was said in England, that the Pope would never have appointed him if he had seen him. Beaumont, however, was a connexion of Edward's queen, Isabella; and John, who was a Provençal, was willing to do anything to oblige the French court. The same year the Pope disregarded both the choice of the chapter of Hereford and the earnest request of the king, and appointed Adam Orlton to the see. Utterly unscrupulous, and at once bold and subtle, Orlton was the worst of all the bad bishops of his time. About two years later, Edward tried to obtain the appointment of Henry Burghersh, the nephew of Lord Badlesmere, who was at that time useful to him, to the see of Winchester. Pope John reserved the see, and appointed an Italian. However, in 1320, the Lincoln chapter elected Burghersh in order to please the king; and Badlesmere, who was then at Avignon, is said to have spent a vast sum of the king's money in procuring the papal assent, for Burghersh was under the canonical age.

When the barons formed a league against the king's favourites, the Despensers, in 1321, they were joined by Burghersh, who followed his kinsman Badlesmere, by Orlton, and John of Drokensford, bishop of Bath. The victory of Boroughbridge gave the king supreme power, and he caused Orlton to be arrested, and charged with treason before the peers. Orlton declared that his metropolitan was, under the Pope, his immediate judge, and refused to plead without the consent of the archbishop and his suffragans. The primate and his suffragans then rose and prayed the king to have mercy on the bishop. Edward refused, and they then pleaded the privilege of the Church, and claimed him as a clerk. He was accordingly delivered over to the custody of the archbishop. Nevertheless the king caused a jury to try him in his absence, and obtained a verdict against him. But the archbishop would not give him up. Edward sent to Avignon to complain of the conduct of the three bishops who had sided with the barons against him, and requested the Pope to deprive them of their English sees. He did not turn his victory to good account. In 1325 two of the bishops who had obtained their sees from the Pope against the king's will, John Stratford of Winchester and William Ayermin of Norwich, while on an embassy to France, entered into a plot against the Despensers. By their advice the queen was sent into France, and there Mortimer joined her. The king in vain urged her to return, and the bishops, at his request, sent a letter to the same effect. She came back at last with an armed force, and Orlton, Burghersh, and Ayermin raised money for her from their fellow-bishops. When she came to Oxford, Orlton expounded the reason of her rebellion to the university in a sermon, taking as his text the words, "Caput meum doleo" (2 Kings iv. 19). Reynolds and some of the bishops remained for a while in London, trying to quiet matters. While they were there, Bishop Stapleton of Exeter, who had been one of the king's ministers, and remained faithful to him, was slain by the citizens. His murder caused them to flee, and Stratford, and at last Reynolds, joined the queen's party. The king was now a prisoner, and Reynolds, who owed everything to his favour, Stratford, whom he had forgiven and trusted in spite of his having deceived him, and Orlton, his avowed enemy, took active part in his deposition.

Meanwhile the province of York had been exposed to the ravages of the Scots. Edward prevailed on John XXII. to command a truce and send over legates with authority to excommunicate Bruce. The legates' envoys were robbed and ill-treated, and the sentence was accordingly pronounced. It had no effect on the war, and in 1318 the Scots broke into Yorkshire. They made a savage raid, and did much damage to churches and ecclesiastical property. Ripon paid them £1000 for its safety. A new archbishop, William Melton, had lately been consecrated. He had served the king and his father well, and Edward, after some trouble, had obtained the Pope's confirmation for him. He was made one of the wardens of the marches, and at once arrayed his tenants for military service. There was little help to be obtained from the king, and when the Scots came down the next year most of the fighting men of the north had been called away to Edward's army at Berwick. Melton, however, raised what local force he could, and led a large and undisciplined host to meet the Scottish army at Myton. The archbishop's army was routed, and so many clerks were slain in the battle that it was called the "chapter of Myton." The absence of any united and vigorous action for the defence of the country was largely due to the disloyalty and selfishness of Thomas, earl of Lancaster. The Sherburn Parliament, 1321. The earl was powerful in Yorkshire, and after making a league for mutual support with the lords of the north, he summoned a meeting of the estates at Sherburn, near Pomfret, in 1321. To this northern parliament he called the archbishop and prelates of the province, and Melton and the clergy obeyed his summons, evidently with the hope of making peace. Lancaster's parliament met in the parish church, and after the schedule of grievances and the lords' bond of association had been read, the earl bade the prelates consult apart, and give him their answer; for all was done as though in a legal and national parliament. The clergy debated in the rectory, and sent a reply in to the earl that was wise and worthy of their profession. They petitioned for a cessation of hostile movements, and for concord in the next parliament, so that, by God's favour, parliament might find remedies for the grievances expressed in the articles. In other words, they exhorted the earl to abandon his isolated position, and seek the good of the country by peaceful and constitutional means. Their answer was received graciously, but their advice was not followed. The archbishop took no part in the disloyal conduct of the majority of the bishops; he and his suffragan of Carlisle, and two bishops of the southern province, protested against the deposition of Edward II., and he abstained from attending the coronation of the young king.

Parliament
and
convocation.

During the reign of Edward II. the clergy showed their unwillingness to attend parliament, and their decided preference for voting their grants in convocation. When, for example, they were summoned to the parliament in which the work of the Ordainers was published in 1311, they sent no proctors.

Before the meeting in the autumn the king wrote to the archbishops, calling on them to urge the attendance of the clergy. Winchelsey objected to the writ, and the king issued another, promising that if it contained any cause of offence it should be remedied. Again, in 1314 Edward ordered the archbishops to summon the convocations of their provinces to treat about an aid. The clergy, however, declared that this was an infringement of the rights of the Church, and departed without further discussion. Before the next parliament, besides the regular writ with the "præmunientes" clause, he sent a special letter to the archbishops, urging them to press the attendance of the clergy; and this double summons was thenceforth sent regularly until 1340. Nevertheless in 1318 the clerical estate in parliament refused to make a grant without convocation. When the matter was referred to the convocation of Canterbury, the answer was returned that the grant must depend on the Pope's consent, and a messenger was sent to Avignon to obtain it. The position of the clerical estate in Parliament was peculiar, for it is certain that its consent was not necessary to legislation. At the same time, when, as in 1316, a petition of the clergy touching spiritual matters received the royal assent, it was with that assent accepted as a statute. In convocation the action of the clergy was perfectly free; they made what grant they would without lay interference, though they had no means of appropriating the supplies they voted. While they withdrew as far as possible from parliament, they did not do so altogether, and in critical times their attendance was specially insisted on, in order that the consent of parliament might be general. Even at the present day they are summoned to every parliament by the "præmunientes" clause, and it is by their own act, by their preference for taxing themselves in their own assembly, that they have lost the right of obeying the summons. Convocations were summoned by the archbishops for other purposes besides taxation, and the ordinary legislative business of the Church was carried on in them. When a convocation met for self-taxation, it did so in consequence of a royal request for money, though it was summoned, as on other occasions, by the archbishop, not by the king. As the king made a like request to the lay estates at the same time, it naturally came to pass that convocation and parliament met about the same date. Nevertheless it would be easy to give many instances which show that meetings of convocation for purposes of taxation were not necessarily concurrent with, nor in any way dependent upon, the parliamentary session, as they became at a later period.

CHAPTER IX.

THE PAPACY AND THE PARLIAMENT.

ECCLESIASTICAL CHARACTER OF THE
REIGN—ARCHBISHOPS AND THEIR
ECCLESIASTICAL
ADMINISTRATION—PROVISIONS—
STATUTE OF PROVISORS—OF
PRÆMUNIRE—REFUSAL OF
TRIBUTE—RELATIONS BETWEEN
THE CHURCH AND THE STATE—
CAUSES OF DISCONTENT AT THE
CONDITION OF THE CHURCH—
ATTACK ON CLERICAL MINISTERS
AND THE WEALTHY CLERGY—
CONCORDAT WITH THE PAPACY—
THE GOOD PARLIAMENT—
CONCLUSION.

Character of
the period.

The fifty years of the reign of Edward III. are of special importance in the history of our Church; for they witnessed the restriction of papal authority by parliament, and the rise of a spirit of discontent at evils which existed in the National Church. From the time of John's submission the Popes had constantly treated England as a never-failing treasury, and had diverted the revenues of the Church to their own purposes. The breach between the papacy and the Crown in the reign of Edward I. had been followed by the expression of the national sense of injury in the parliament of Carlisle. The war with France caused the anti-papal feeling to grow and bring forth fruit. It was intolerable that the wealth of the country should go to enrich its enemies, and that French Popes should exercise jurisdiction here in defiance of the will of the king and to the subversion of the common law. The victories of England find their ecclesiastical significance in the legislation against papal oppression, in the statutes of Provisors and Præmunire. Within the Church several causes combined to give rise to an anti-clerical feeling. While the nation suffered severely from the expenses of the war, the Church was rich, and might, so men thought, well be forced to bear a larger share of the general burdens than the clergy were willing to lay upon themselves. The bishops filled all the chief administrative offices, and enjoyed their revenues in

122

addition to the wealth of their sees. The inferior clergy were as a rule careless and ignorant. The Church, though it jealously watched over its rights of jurisdiction, found itself powerless to enforce needful discipline on the clergy, while the abuses of the ecclesiastical courts were a continual source of irritation to the laity. An attempt was made to debar the prelates from political offices, and an attack on the wealth of the Church was threatened. Then came the papal Schism, and new ideas were openly expressed concerning the papacy itself, the position and rights of the clergy, and the relations between Church and State. With these ideas we have nothing to do here. But as we follow the ecclesiastical history of the reign we shall see how the way was prepared for them; how it was that Wyclif, a strenuous upholder of the rights of the National Church, was led to form a spiritual conception of the Church Universal, to declare that a Pope who was not Christ-like was Antichrist, and to teach that it would be well for the Church to strip herself of her endowments and to become independent of the State; why it was that the bulwarks already raised against papal interference were strengthened, and why for a season there were from time to time evidences of a spirit of revolt against the ecclesiastical system. It will perhaps be convenient to divide the Church history of the reign into two unequal parts at the return of the Prince of Wales and the meeting of the anti-clerical parliament in 1371, and after some notices of the archbishops and their ecclesiastical administration down to the consecration of Whittlesey in 1368, to take a survey of the relations, first, between the papacy and England, and, secondly, between the National Church and the State during that period, and to end with some account of the anti-clerical movement of the last years of the reign.

Simon
Mepeham,
archbishop
of
Canterbury,
1328-1333.

On the death of Reynolds in 1327, the Canterbury chapter elected Simon Mepeham, and at Queen Isabella's request, and after receiving a gift from the convent, John XXII. confirmed the election. Mepeham was a scholar and a theologian. He held councils, published canons, and did what he could to rule well. Conscious of the necessity of reform, he set about a provincial visitation, and fined and excommunicated the bishop of Rochester for non-residence, neglect of duty, and laxity of government. When he came to Exeter, Bishop Grandison, who built a large part of the cathedral there, refused to receive him, and drew up his men under arms to oppose his entrance. Grandison, who claimed a papal exemption from metropolitan visitation, appealed to the Pope, and the king ordered the archbishop to desist from his attempt. This seems to have brought his efforts for reformation, which excited much ill-will among his suffragans, to a premature end. He was involved in a quarrel with the monks of St. Augustine's, who also resisted his authority. They appealed to the Pope, and Mepeham, who refused to give way, died under excommunication.

John Stratford, archbishop of Canterbury, 1333-1348.

John Stratford, bishop of Winchester, of whom we have heard before, was at the king's instance elected to succeed him, and the Pope provided him, not in virtue of the postulation of the chapter, but "of his own motion." Although the chapter of Winchester elected, and the king recommended, the prior of Worcester as Stratford's successor, Orlton, who happened to be at Avignon, was, on the recommendation of Philip of France, provided by the Pope to the vacant see. The king was indignant, and called on Orlton to answer for thus procuring the papal brief against his will, but let the matter drop. Edward's ministers were mostly churchmen, and for about eleven years after the fall of Mortimer, Stratford, or his brother, the bishop of Chichester, generally held the office of chancellor, and exerted themselves to raise money for the French war. For some years Edward made no progress in the war, and was generally unsuccessful except at sea. Stratford, who belonged to the old Lancastrian party, disapproved of the constant waste of money, and recommended peace. Money on which the king reckoned was not forthcoming, and in 1340, excited probably by the misrepresentations of the court party, and especially by Bishops Burghersh and Orlton, he returned suddenly to England, turned Stratford's brother, the chancellor, and other ministers out of office, and imprisoned some of his judges and other officers. His controversy with the king. Stratford was summoned to appear at court, but retired to Canterbury, and there preached some sermons, the character of which may be judged by the text of one of them: "He was not moved with the presence of any prince, neither could any bring him into subjection" (Ecclus. xlviii. 12). He further excommunicated all who offered violence to clerks or accused them falsely to the king. Edward replied by putting forth a pamphlet containing his complaints against the archbishop. In this pamphlet, which is called the *famosus libellus*, he charged Stratford with being the cause of his want of success by keeping him short of funds in order to gain profit for himself, and added several accusations which were mere abuse. Although Orlton denied it, this discreditable document was probably drawn up by him. Stratford answered it point by point, and complained that the king was condemning him, one of the chief peers of the realm, without trial. Edward carried on this paper war with another weak letter, and wrote to Benedict XII., complaining of the archbishop, and hinting that he wished the Pope to suspend him. When parliament met in the spring of 1341, various attempts were made to prevent the archbishop from taking his seat, and the king began proceedings against him in the Exchequer. Stratford persisted in appearing in parliament, and offered to plead before his peers. The lords thereupon declared that no peer should be brought to trial except before his peers in parliament. Edward found it advisable to be reconciled to the archbishop, and the struggle ended. The archbishop's persistence thus led to the establishment of the most important privilege of the peerage, and the result of the controversy illustrates the constitutional position of bishops as of equal dignity with the temporal lords. A lay chancellor, 1340.Meanwhile the king appointed Sir Robert Bourchier chancellor, the first layman who ever held that office. After a little time, however, the office was again held by clerks.

Stratford desired good government, and the clergy under his rule on one occasion joined the other estates in demanding redress of grievances, asking, for their part, that the charters should be confirmed, as well as that their own privileges of jurisdiction should be better observed: yet he made no real effort to secure constitutional liberty. His constitutions.Although more of a statesman than an archbishop, he was fully alive to the evils arising from the oppressions of the ecclesiastical officials and the secular lives of the clergy, and held two councils, in which he regulated the officials' fees, forbade bishops and archdeacons, when on a visitation, to quarter a large retinue on the clergy, ordered that archdeacons should not make a gain of commutations for corporal penance, and that clerks who concealed their tonsure, had long curled hair, and imitated the dress of laymen by wearing knives, long shoes, and furred cloaks, should be suspended.

Battle of
Nevill's
Cross, 18th
October
1345.

Meanwhile William Zouche, archbishop of York, was engaged in the defence of his province. In October 1345, while Edward was absent in France, David of Scotland led a large army into the bishopric of Durham, wasting the country as he advanced. Archbishop William and the lords Nevill and Percy raised a force, in which, along with knights and men-at-arms, were many of the northern clergy, the archbishop in person leading one of the divisions. The English gained a signal victory at Nevill's Cross; the Scottish king was taken prisoner, and the "chapter of Myton" was amply avenged.

John of

On Stratford's death in 1348 the monks of Christ Church, thinking to please the king, and doubtless also to found a precedent, elected Edward's chaplain, Thomas Bradwardine, without waiting for the *congé d'elire*. Bradwardine, the *Doctor Profundus*, as he was called, a famous philosopher and theologian, was the champion of the Augustinian doctrine of predestination against the Scotists. He had accompanied the king in his victorious campaigns against France, and had been employed by him to treat of peace. Edward, though he was willing enough that he should be archbishop, would not allow the chapter to act independently, and so caused Clement VI. to provide his chancellor, John Ufford, who was an aged man. The pestilence now reached England, and Ufford died of it before he was consecrated. Thomas Bradwardine, archbishop of Canterbury, 1349. Bradwardine was then raised to the archbishopric by the common action of the king, the chapter, and the Pope; for after the English victories Clement was ready to oblige Edward, declaring that "if the king of England asked a bishopric for an ass he could not refuse him." His subservience to Edward displeased the cardinals, and at the consecration feast of the great English doctor at Avignon one of them sent into the hall a buffoon mounted on an ass, with a petition that the Pope would make him archbishop of Canterbury. A week after Bradwardine came to England he too died of the pestilence, which both now and in its later outbreaks fell as heavily on the clergy as on the laity, carrying off four bishops in a single year.

Simon Islip, Bradwardine's successor, endeavoured to remedy ecclesiastical abuses. He founded Canterbury Hall at Oxford, to enable the clergy to receive a better education, and published some excellent constitutions in convocation. Clerical offenders claimed by the Church from the secular courts, and committed to the custody of the bishops, were often kept in comfort; they sometimes escaped from their prisons, and sometimes were released without good cause. This was no longer to be; and imprisonment was to be made a real punishment. The archbishop also decreed that chaplains who were engaged to perform commemorative masses should, if required, be bound to do parochial work at a fixed stipend of one mark beyond their ordinary pay, which he fixed at five marks. A long-standing dispute between the sees of Canterbury and York as to the right of the northern metropolitan to carry his cross erect in the southern province was at last settled by an agreement between Islip and John Thoresby, archbishop of York. When the king and the parliament checked the papal aggressions Islip abstained from interference; for, while he could not quarrel with the papacy, he would not uphold it against the will of the nation. While, however, he was prudent and moderate in temper, he did not shrink from speaking plainly on behalf of good government, and wrote a strong remonstrance to the king about the oppression of the people by the royal purveyors. Simon Langham, 1366-1368. On Islip's death Simon Langham, bishop of Ely, was raised to the primacy. He was chancellor when he was translated, but did not hold the office long afterwards. By the command of Pope Urban V. he instituted an inquiry into cases of plurality, and found that some clerks held as many as twenty benefices by provisions, with license to add to their number. After he had held the archbishopric two years, Urban made him a cardinal. The king was displeased at this, and seized his temporalities. William Whittlesey, archbishop, 1368-1374. Langham resigned the see and went to Avignon, and was succeeded at Canterbury by his kinsman, William Whittlesey, who took little part in the affairs either of Church or State, for he soon fell into ill health.

The Church
 and the
 Papacy,
1327-1371.

There was comparatively little direct taxation of the clergy by the Popes during this reign, though first-fruits were still demanded, and the frequency with which promotions were effected by provision probably led to a growing compliance with the demand. At the same time, the Church was wronged in a more mischievous manner by the Popes' usurpation of patronage. English bishoprics, dignities, and cures were conferred without regard to the fitness of the person promoted, and simply as a matter of policy, or a means of providing for the friends and advisers of the Pope. The first decided check that was administered to this abuse arose from the war with France; for it was felt to be intolerable that the wealth of the country should be handed over to the French cardinals and other members of the papal court at Avignon. During the early years of the reign little resistance was offered to the system of appointment by provision, though two sees, Exeter and Bath, which had been reserved, were filled up by the joint action of the Crown and the chapters. Reservations and provisions. The abuse grew rapidly, until, in 1343, Clement VI. declared that he had reserved benefices, not including bishoprics, as they fell vacant, to the annual value of 2000 marks for two cardinals, who sent their agents to England to carry out their claims. These agents were ordered to depart, on pain of imprisonment, and a complaint was made to the Crown by the lay estates in parliament that the richest benefices in the country were bestowed by the Pope on foreigners, who never came near it, or contributed to its burdens, and who abstracted the wealth of England to the prejudice of the king and his kingdom, and, above all, of the souls of his subjects. The bishops did not dare to join in this complaint, and wished to withdraw, but the king made them stay during the proceedings. In answer to this complaint, a royal ordinance was published that any one who brought bulls or reservations into the kingdom should be imprisoned. Resisted by the king and parliament. Moreover, the king wrote a letter to the Pope representing that provisions led to the promotion of unfit persons, who did not understand the language of the country or reside on their benefices, and that they robbed patrons and chapters of their rights, and removed cases of patronage from the royal to the papal courts. A vigorous letter of remonstrance was also sent by the parliament by the hands of John of Shoreditch, a famous lawyer, who presented it to the Pope in the presence of the cardinals. Clement was angry, and declared he had only provided two foreigners. "Holy Father," John replied, "you have provided the Cardinal of Perigord to the deanery of York, and the king and all the nobles of England know him to be a capital enemy of the king and kingdom." High words passed; the cardinals left the court in some confusion, and John departed from Avignon in haste, lest mischief should befall him.

Statute of
Provisors,
1351.

These remonstrances had little effect, and at last, in 1351, the statute of Provisors was enacted, on the petition of the lords temporal and the commons. By this statute any collation made by the Pope was to escheat to the Crown, and any person acting in virtue of a reservation or provision was, after conviction, to be imprisoned until he had paid such fine as the king might inflict, and had made compensation to the party aggrieved. To this statute the bishops, who were, of course, hampered by their position as regards the Pope, did not assent. Its immediate effect was rather to strengthen the hold of the king upon the Church than to increase its liberty. Edward connived at its evasion whenever it suited him to do so, and infringed the rights of patrons by a writ called "Quare impedit," while the concurrence of the Popes, who took care to keep on good terms with the victorious king, enabled him to do much as he liked. The Popes, moreover, still continued to provide to sees vacant by translation, and accordingly multiplied translations to the hurt of the Church. It was found necessary to re-enact the penalties of the statute fourteen years later, and, as we shall see, fresh efforts were made against the abuse towards the end of the reign.

The system of provisions increased the number of appeals to Rome, and matters that were determinable at common law were carried to the Pope's court, much to the inconvenience of the parties concerned, and to the profit of the papal officers. Statute of Præmunire, 1353. In 1353 a check was given to the appellate jurisdiction of the curia by the Statute of Præmunire, which, without verbal reference to the Pope, made it punishable with imprisonment and forfeiture to draw one of the king's subjects out of the kingdom to answer in a foreign court, the offender being compelled to appear by a writ beginning "Præmunire facias." This statute was re-enacted in 1365, with distinct mention of the Roman court; the prelates protesting, evidently for form's sake, that they would assent to nothing that was injurious to the Church. Although the Pope still granted dispensations from the canon law, and his jurisdiction might still be invoked in cases for which no remedy was provided at common law, papal interference in legal matters of importance now became rare. New statutes of Provisors and Præmunire were promulgated in the next reign.

The victories of Edward and the Prince of Wales rendered the Popes powerless to resent anti-papal legislation. France was no longer able to protect them at Avignon. During their residence in that city the papacy had become French, and had consequently in a large measure lost its hold upon England. Repudiation of vassalage, 1366. Urban V. unwisely provoked a declaration that bore witness to this decline of influence. He wrote to Edward demanding the arrears of the tribute promised by John, and threatened to cite the king if he neglected payment. Edward laid the demand before the parliament that met in May 1366, and requested the advice of the estates. The prelates, speaking for themselves, asked for a day for deliberation. The next day the three estates separately and unanimously declared that John had no power to bring his realm and people under such subjection, and repudiated the vassalage and tribute that the Pope demanded. For a short time Edward stopped even the payment of Peter's pence.

The Church
in relation
to the State,
1327-1371.
Taxation.
Legislation.

Early in the reign the Pope granted the king a clerical tenth for four years, and later, during the French war, the clergy taxed themselves heavily. All attempt to induce them to make their grants in parliament was discontinued, and they settled the amount of their contribution in their provincial convocations. In convocation they legislated without interference on spiritual matters, including those which concerned their jurisdiction. Parliament, however, did not allow them to enact anything that should bind the laity without its consent. Accordingly, when Stratford published a constitution on the right to the tithe of underwood, a petition was the next year presented by the commons, praying that the Crown would not grant any petition of the clergy that might prejudice the laity without examination; for, though the clergy legislated on the process for recovery of tithes, parliament claimed to determine their incidence. This distinction found its counterpart in jurisdiction; for the common law courts decided questions of right to tithes, while the spiritual courts enforced payment. In matters affecting temporal interests, parliament legislated for the Church. This legislation was during this period generally of a favourable character, and was founded on petitions from the clergy. Parliament, for example, declared by statute that the temporalities of bishops were not to be seized except according to the law of the land and after judgment, and that during a vacancy they were to be carefully and honestly administered. Again, as the pestilence raised the price of clerical as well as of all other labour, parliament in 1362 represented that chaplains had become scarce and dear, and prayed that they might be compelled to work for lower pay than they were in the habit of receiving. The king ordered the bishops to find a remedy; and they reported Islip's constitution, which was thus turned into a parliamentary statute, a kind of "Statute of Labourers" for the unbeneficed clergy. Jurisdiction. Disputes still went on as to rights of jurisdiction, and in 1344, after the grant of a clerical tenth, it was enacted, with the assent of the lay estates, that the ecclesiastical courts should not be subject to unfair interference either by writs of prohibition or by inquiry by secular judges; the whole statute forming a kind of reading of "Circumspecte agatis" in the clerical interest.

Discontent
of the laity.

Nevertheless the nation regarded the condition of the Church with growing discontent. The papal interference with the rights of patrons, besides grievously wronging the bishops and chapters, irritated the people at large, for they saw ecclesiastical offices and revenues held by foreigners who never set foot in England, and were in many cases their enemies. Of this perhaps enough has been said. Non-residence. Non-residence and plurality, however, were not confined to foreigners. All the great offices of State were, as a rule, held by bishops and other dignified clergy, who neglected their ecclesiastical for their civil duties; and the inferior clergy followed their example, and engaged in secular employments of all kinds. Non-residence was increased by the pestilence. Much land fell out of cultivation, and so ceased to yield tithes, and parsons left their parishes whenever they could obtain some profitable work to do elsewhere. So the poet of Piers Ploughman records how—

> Parsons and parisshe preestes
> That hire parisshes weren povere
> To have a licence and leve
> And syngen ther for symonie;

Somme serven the kyng
In cheker and in chauncelrie
Of wardes and of wardmotes
And somme serven as servauntz
And in stede of stywardes

Pleyned hem to the bisshope,
Sith the pestilence tyme,
At London to dwelle,
For silver is swete.

And his silver tellen
Chalangan his dettes
Weyves and streyves.
Lordes and ladies,
Sitten and demen.

In the absence of the parish priests, or while they were immersed in worldly affairs, the churches fell into decay, and the people were neglected. Secular employments.Wyclif tells us that secular employment was the only road to ecclesiastical preferment. "Lords," he says, "wolen not present a clerk able of kunning of God's law, but a kitchen clerk, or a peny clerk, or wise in building castles or worldly doing, though he kunne not reade wel his sauter." Clergy such as these held a vast number of preferments, for the Pope readily granted dispensations for plurality. William of Wykeham, the king's architect, afterwards bishop of Winchester, held at one time, while Keeper of the Privy Seal, the archdeaconry of Lincoln and eleven prebends in various churches.

Lack of discipline. Oppression of the spiritual courts. Decline in the general character of the clergy. Efforts to raise their character.

The spiritual jurisdiction for which churchmen contended so jealously had altogether failed to preserve discipline. The secularization of the clergy rendered this failure specially disastrous; for a clerk, who had laid aside everything clerical except the tonsure, and had perhaps concealed that, if accused of any crime, however grave, was immediately claimed by his order, and was only amenable to a law that was powerless to inflict an adequate punishment for the worst offences. Nor were clerical offenders rare, for the number of those in orders of one kind or another was very large. Many of them had little to do, their duties merely consisting in the performance of anniversary services, and so, being idle, they were prone to self-indulgence and mischief. Several of the archbishops of Canterbury endeavoured, as we have seen, to restore discipline, but the spiritual courts were corrupt, and their efforts were of little avail. Yet, while the laity saw discipline utterly broken down, they found the spiritual courts strong enough to oppress them with heavy fees, especially in testamentary cases, and in various other ways, and the cost and vexation entailed by ecclesiastical processes were a constant source of irritation. At the same time, high as the pretensions of the clergy were, there can be no doubt that the clerical standard was lowered by the pestilence. Many benefices were suddenly vacated, and there were few to fill them. The ranks of the clergy must have been recruited with men of inferior education, and it was by them that the vacant cures were supplied. Some efforts were made to remedy the ignorance of those who should have been the teachers of the people. Islip's foundation at Oxford has already been noticed; it was soon to be followed by the more magnificent foundations of William of Wykeham. Meanwhile, in the north, the most backward part of the kingdom, Archbishop Thoresby, a prelate of noble character, laboured to bring about a better state of things. He constantly visited different parts of his diocese, teaching, and correcting abuses, and in order that his people might know the elements of Christianity, he published a kind of catechism in two versions, one in Latin for the clergy, whose ignorance and carelessness he severely reprehended, and the other in English verse for the laity.

Discontent at the condition of the Church grew bitter as the people at large felt the burden of a war that had ceased to be glorious, and the general decline in prosperity aggravated the religious disaffection. Men saw with anger that, while the nation groaned under heavy taxation, the greater ecclesiastics held all the richest offices in the State as well as in the Church, and that, large as their revenues were, the country was misgoverned and the war mismanaged. Attack on the clerical ministers and the wealthy clergy, 1371. An anti-clerical party arose, and an attack was made on ecclesiastical ministers and the wealthier churchmen. When the Prince of Wales returned from Aquitaine, in January 1371, fresh supplies were demanded of parliament. In reply, the lay estates presented a petition complaining that the government had too long been in the hands of the clergy, who could not be called to account, and requesting that the king would consider that laymen were fit to be employed in offices of state. In consequence of this petition, the chancellor, William of Wykeham, and the treasurer, the bishop of Exeter, resigned, and their places were taken by laymen. An attempt of the monastic orders to claim exemption from the payment of subsidies led to some bitter words concerning the wealth of the greater churchmen. A lord compared the Church to an owl that was unfledged until each bird gave it a feather to deck itself with; suddenly, he said, a hawk appeared, and the birds demanded back their feathers in order that they might escape. The owl refused; so they stripped him, and flew away in safety, leaving him in worse plight than he was before. Even so, he continued, in this dangerous war ought we to take back from the wealthy clergy the temporalities which belong to us and to the realm, and defend the realm with these our own goods rather than by increased taxation. The clergy took the hint, and promised the Prince of Wales in convocation to grant £50,000, a sum to which even those whose endowments had hitherto escaped on account of their smallness were obliged to contribute. John of Gaunt returned the next year, and probably took the lead of the anti-clerical party, in opposition to the Prince of Wales, who upheld William of Wykeham. Although this year an attack was made in parliament on the lawyers, the abuses of the Church did not escape. Petitions were presented requesting that the king would confiscate the revenues of foreign beneficed clergy who did not live in the kingdom— this was refused; that bishops' officials should demand less exorbitant fees in testamentary cases—in this matter the bishops were ordered to find a remedy; and that the benefices of clergy who lived in open concubinage should, if the bishop neglected to act, become *ipso facto* void, and that the Crown should present—to this no answer was returned.

When John of Gaunt came back from his unsuccessful campaign in 1373 his influence in parliament was lessened. Nevertheless a petition was presented against the encroachments of the clerical courts. A strong remonstrance was also made on the subject of reservations and provisions and on the withdrawal of money from the country by foreign ecclesiastics. Concordat with the Pope. To this the king replied that he had already sent an embassy to the Pope to represent these grievances, probably in consequence of the petition of the year before, and the matter was referred to a conference about to be held at Bruges. When the king's demand for a tenth was laid before convocation by Archbishop Whittlesey, the clergy declared that they were undone by the exactions of the Pope and the king, and that they could better help the king "if the intolerable yoke of the Pope were taken from their necks;" and Courtenay, bishop of Hereford, protested that he would not consent to the grant unless some remedy were devised for these evils. The tenth was, however, granted, and all looked for what the negotiations at Bruges would bring forth. Conference at Bruges, 1374-1375. To this conference, which met the following year, Edward sent the bishop of Bangor, Dr. John Wyclif, and others, as his representatives to arrange a concordat with Gregory XI. The immediate results, which were declared in 1375, were unsatisfactory, for they were merely temporary in their application. However, in 1377, the king's jubilee year, Edward announced that the Pope had promised that he would abstain from reservations; that he would not provide to any bishopric until sufficient time had elapsed for him to hear the result of the capitular election; that he would respect the elective rights of other capitular bodies; that he would diminish the number of foreign ecclesiastics; that though he would not give up his claim to first-fruits, which were still held to be an innovation, he would see that they did not press too heavily on the clergy; and that he would be moderate in issuing expectatives and provisions.

The Good
Parliament,
    1376.

No parliament met from 1373 until the Good Parliament of 1376. In this parliament the party of reform was upheld by the Prince of Wales and the bishop of Winchester. The Prince of Wales died during the session of the parliament, and left the leaders of the party exposed to the vengeance of John of Gaunt. A series of accusations was brought against Wykeham, his temporalities were seized, and he was forbidden to come near the court. Accordingly, he did not come up to the convocation of 1377, and Simon Sudbury, the archbishop of Canterbury, refused to specially request his attendance. His opposition was overruled by Courtenay, now bishop of London, who dwelt on the injustice that had been done Wykeham by the Crown, and urged the clergy to make no grant until he joined them. Wykeham came up to convocation, and the king promised to redress his wrongs. And here, at the point at which the quarrel assumes a new phase, when the clergy were about to aim a blow at their enemy, John of Gaunt, by attacking his ally, John Wyclif, at the opening of strife between Lollardy and the Church, and at the beginning of a new era in the relations between Rome and the English and other national Churches, brought about by the papal Schism, this narrative reaches its appointed limit.

Summary,
601-1066.
  601-664.

Each period of the history we have been studying has some special characteristics, and it may be convenient to sum them up briefly. The partial failure of the Kentish mission and the break-down of Gregory's scheme of government left the English Church in a disorganized condition, and Rome had to win a second victory to save it from Celtic customs and separation from the rest of Christendom. The hero of that victory was Wilfrith, its token the restoration of the see of York. A new period opens with the work of Theodore, and extends from the victory of the Roman party at Whitby to the end of the greatness of the Northumbrian Church, and the establishment of the sovereignty of Wessex. 663-829.The diocesan scheme of Theodore succeeded, and is the basis of our present arrangement. His attempt to bring the whole Church under the rule of a single metropolitan failed, for the northern Church was for a season more advanced than the rest of the land in religion and culture; and its failure is marked by the restoration of the see of York to metropolitan rank. From the first the Church was national in character, independent of the rise and fall of the petty kingdoms into which the land was divided, and it became a powerful agent in the accomplishment of national unity. Nor was it by any means a handmaid of Rome, for the attempt of Wilfrith to regain his position by invoking the papal authority met with derision and defeat. From the first, too, the Church and the civil power worked in complete harmony, and when national unity was attained, the Church bore its own share in every department of the polity it had done so much to create. For a moment, indeed, its work in teaching the lesson of union was threatened by the baleful predominance of Mercia; for the foundation of the Mercian archiepiscopate was an attempt to make the Church minister to the greatness of a single kingdom; its failure saved her from degradation, and probably saved the nation from prolonged division. By Archbishop Ceolnoth's alliance with Ecgberht, the Church adopted the interests of the line of kings under whom the unity of the nation was accomplished.

829-988.

While the invasion of the Northmen completed the ruin of the northern church, Alfred and his son imparted new vigour to the life of the southern province, and their work was carried further forward by the great churchmen whose names are connected with the monastic revival of the tenth century. This period of recovery may be said to close with the death of Dunstan. Although the relations between England and Rome became more intimate under the immediate successors of Ecgberht, and especially under Alfred, the work of restoration was not due to direct Roman influence; it was effected mainly through intercourse with France, Flanders, and Germany. Throughout the period the unity of action of the Church and State is strongly marked; separate conciliar action became rare, and both spiritual and secular affairs were administered by statesmen-bishops. 988-1066.During the first part of the eleventh century this union became even more intimate, greatly to the loss of the Church; for the bishops were absorbed in worldly matters and party strife. Freedom from Roman interference and a long course of independent and purely national life, however good in themselves, proved dangerous, for the Church had not yet attained any widespread culture.

Summary,
1066-1135.

The conquest of England may be regarded as a papal triumph over a Church and a nation which had stood apart from Roman Christendom and followed their own devices. Both before and after his victory the Conqueror availed himself of the help of Rome. Nevertheless he was strong enough to hold his own even against Gregory VII., and refused to allow the Pope any authority in his kingdom excepting within limits of his own appointment. The Church equally with the nation was conquered, and tasted the bitterness of defeat, but there was no break in the continuity of its life. Each Norman or French bishop who succeeded to the see of an English predecessor looked on himself as an English bishop, and the Church of the conquered people united conquerors and conquered in one English nation. William strengthened the Church as a means of strengthening himself, and his policy of separating the spiritual and secular courts was followed by few signs of coming conflict during the strong rule of the Norman kings.

1139-1205.

The conflict came after a suspension of the royal authority. The immunity of the clergy from secular jurisdiction confronted Henry II. as a dangerous obstacle to the success of his designs for the foundation of a strong and orderly government. His strife with Archbishop Thomas ended in his humiliation, but it left in the Constitutions of Clarendon the groundwork of a system to which the future relations between Church and State made continual and progressive approaches. The Church lost by the dispute; for the energy that might have been devoted to producing a higher clerical standard was frittered in a somewhat ignoble quarrel. Yet it also gained something besides a victory of doubtful benefit. Anselm, in a better cause, had already resisted despotism; and Thomas died for what he believed to be the rights of the Church over which he had been called to rule. Both alike asserted the sacredness of spiritual things. Neither Anselm nor Thomas received any hearty support from Rome; in both cases the action of the Popes appears to have been governed by motives of expediency. Nor was it in the Church's quarrel alone that churchmen dared to encounter the wrath of kings. Thomas of Canterbury, Hugh of Lincoln, and Geoffrey of York each opposed the undue exercise of the royal power in secular matters, and were the earliest assertors of constitutional rights. At the same time, under both the Norman and the first two Plantagenet kings, the Church at large was on the side of the

136

Crown, and did the nation good service by maintaining its authority against the feudal nobility.

1205-1265.

The quarrel between John and Innocent III. introduces a new period in our history, during which the Church was in opposition to the Crown, and was contending for national liberties against the king and his suzerain, the Pope. Although, as the vassal of Innocent, the king was upheld by all the power that the greatest of the Popes could exert, the Church cast in its lot with the nation, and took a foremost part in winning the Great Charter. It paid dearly for its self-devotion. Innocent had, however, overreached himself, for his attempt to uphold his vassal against the liberties of the country roused a bitter feeling against the papacy; and this feeling was deepened as succeeding Popes took advantage of the weakness of Henry III. to grind down the Church and oppress the country in order to raise funds for their war with the Hohenstaufen house. In the resistance that was at last made to the king's misgovernment the Church was again foremost in the cause of liberty, while the Pope again upheld his vassal against his people. The barons' war, however, virtually brought the papal suzerainty to an end.

A decisive blow was given to the power of the Popes in England by the folly of Boniface VIII., who forced Edward I. into hostility, and so made the Crown at one with the people in resisting papal pretensions. Nor were the clergy whole-hearted on the Popes' side, for they had learned by bitter experience that they would at least gain nothing by the victory of Rome. Almost as soon, then, as the machinery for the expression of the national will was perfected, the king and the nation used it to express their indignation at the usurpations of the papacy. 1272-1307.The reign is further memorable in ecclesiastical history for the king's work in defining the position of the Church in relation to the State. The policy of making the clergy a parliamentary estate so far failed that they succeeded in withdrawing themselves from parliament and making their grants in convocation, yet the attempt to secure their attendance brought their action in fiscal matters into correspondence with, though not into dependence upon, the action of the other estates of the realm. In matters of jurisdiction, Edward's rule contained in the writ "Circumspecte agatis" was founded on clear and well-considered principles, and became the groundwork of all future legislation on the subject in mediæval times. In all points the Church was given an ascertained place in the national system, and while the king exacted many heavy taxes from the clergy, and occasionally, when it suited his convenience, made use of the papal authority, he never gave way to any attempt of Pope or archbishop to act as though the clergy had separate interests from the nation at large. For our purpose, the reign of his unhappy son is important mainly as exhibiting how entirely the success of the policy of

137

Edward I. was the result of his personal character. 1307-1327.The weakness of Edward II. gave the Popes a chance of which they did not fail to avail themselves. While wholly under French influence, they did not hesitate to treat the English Church as arrogantly as they had treated it in the days when the papacy was strong. Under Edward I. the chapters virtually lost the power of electing bishops; during the reign of his son the will of the Crown was constantly set at nought, and the introduction of the system of reservation and provision as applied to bishoprics indicates the utter disregard with which the rights both of the Church and the king were treated at Avignon.

1343-1377.

A new and powerful motive for resistance was supplied by the French war of Edward III. Parliament and the Crown were at one in refusing to yield to papal pretensions, and the first statutes of Provisors and Præmunire, though they by no means put a stop to the evils at which they were aimed, at least taught the Popes the necessity of moderation. We leave the Church in the midst of a struggle. Exhausted with the burden of the French war, and disappointed at the change from victory to defeat, the nation was inclined to find fault with existing institutions. The wealth and power of the Church provoked envy; its abuses were regarded with indignation. The earliest phase of the struggle, the attack made in Parliament upon the clerical ministers and the richer clergy, brings this volume to a close. The work and theories of Wyclif and his followers, and the effects of the papal schism on the relations between England and Rome, are reserved for another volume of this series.

THE END.

Ingram Content Group UK Ltd.
Milton Keynes UK
UKHW012120060323
418148UK00003B/90

9 783752 383379